D0948068

RECLUSE

WOLFES OF MANHATTAN TWO

HELEN HARDT

RECLUSE
WOLFES OF MANHATTAN TWO

by
Helen Hardt

HARDT & SONS ♥

🌸 Created with Vellum

For my readers

A secret lies trapped in the deepest recesses of Roy Wolfe's mind.

And it's slowly drowning him.

When Charlene Waters's boss married the new CEO of Wolfe Enterprises after a whirlwind romance, she brought her assistant along for the ride. Charlie now has a cushy new job at the billion dollar company, and she's excited to begin her new venture.

Roy Wolfe is a recluse. He's never taken an active role in his family's business, and he has no desire to now. He's only in the office to deal with the fallout from his father's murder. He, along with the rest of his siblings, have all been implicated. Meeting Charlie Waters with the gorgeous silver eyes complicates things. Their chemistry is immediate and passionate, but he can't be what she deserves.

Roy knows his father was hiding something even more sinister than his brothers and sister can imagine—something he witnessed years ago that he can't bring to his conscious mind.

But he must—for Charlie, and for his family. Or they may all pay the ultimate price.

PRAISE FOR HELEN HARDT

STEEL BROTHERS SAGA

"Craving is the jaw-dropping book you *need* to read!"
~ Lisa Renee Jones, *New York Times* bestselling author

"Completely raw and addictive."
~ Meredith Wild, #1 *New York Times* bestselling author

"Talon has hit my top five list...up there next to Jamie Fraser and Gideon Cross."
~ Angel Payne, *USA Today* bestselling author

"Talon is a sexy, intriguing leading man and Jade, our lady left at the altar is a sweet and relatable girl you just want to hug. Together they build a steaming hot relationship you really root for from the first chapter!"
-CD Reiss, *New York Times* bestselling author

"Talon and Jade's instant chemistry heats up the pages..."
~ RT Book Reviews

"Sorry Christian and Gideon, there's a new heartthrob for you to contend with. Meet Talon. Talon Steel."

~ **Booktopia**

"Such a beautiful torment—the waiting, the anticipation, the relief that only comes briefly before more questions arise, and the wait begins again... Check. Mate. Ms. Hardt..."

~ **Bare Naked Words**

"Made my heart stop in my chest. Helen has given us such a heartbreakingly beautiful series."

~**Tina, Bookalicious Babes**

BLOOD BOND SAGA

"An enthralling and rousing vampire tale that will leave readers waiting for the sequel."

~ **Kirkus Reviews**

"Helen gives us the dark, tormented vampire hero we all love in a sensual paranormal romance with all the feels. Be warned... The twists and turns will keep you up all night reading. I was hooked from the first sentence until the very end."

~ **J.S. Scott,** *New York Times* **bestselling author**

"A dark, intoxicating tale."

~ **Library Journal**

"Helen dives into the paranormal world of vampires and makes it her own."

~ **Tina, Bookalicious Babes**

"Throw out everything you know about vampires—except for that blood thirst we all love and lust after in these stunning heroes—and expect to be swept up in a sensual story that twists and turns in so many wonderfully jaw-dropping ways."
~ **Angel Payne, USA Today bestselling author**

WOLFES OF MANHATTAN

"It's hot, it's intense, and the plot starts off thick and had me completely spellbound from page one."
~ **The Sassy Nerd Blog**

Helen Hardt...is a master at her craft.
~**K. Ogburn, Amazon**

Move over Steel brothers... Rock is *everything!*
~**Barbara Conklin-Jaros, Amazon**

Helen has done it again. She winds you up and weaves a web of intrigue.
~**Vicki Smith, Amazon**

WARNING

The Wolfes of Manhattan series contains adult language and scenes, including flashbacks of child physical and sexual abuse. Please take note.

PROLOGUE
ROY

The secret had lodged in my gut, always present, sometimes churning, and occasionally clawing its way up my throat as acidic bile, eating through my flesh.

For most of my life I'd ignored it. Not like I hadn't had years to tamp it down, pretend it didn't exist. Days had begun to pass where I didn't think about it. Days turned into weeks, into months, eventually into years.

But always it was there, like a black cancer haunting me from the inside out.

Who to trust?

I was a recluse, never close to anyone, really—certainly not anyone in my family.

Flying to Montana to talk to Rock had been a mistake. I couldn't expose my secret with his girlfriend there—his girlfriend who was a lawyer, for God's sake.

Now I existed in a perpetual cold sweat, trapped in the ultimate mindfuck.

Help me. Please. Help me.

1

CHARLIE

My new employer was Wolfe Enterprises.

Seriously.

A new position, a new title, a posh new office, and a hefty raise in pay.

Life was good.

Moving over to the Wolfe Plaza Tower was easier than I'd ever imagined. Everything stayed. I gathered only my few personal items to take with me to my new office. Yes, I'd have my own office!

I'd been the assistant to Lacey Ward since she became an associate at the law firm. She hired me herself. I was fresh out of paralegal school and green as they come. That was six years ago. Lacey was the youngest attorney ever to make partner at our prestigious Manhattan firm...and now she was leaving.

For good reason.

Rock Wolfe was the CEO of Wolfe Enterprises. He was also Lacey's new husband. They'd met, fallen in love, and gotten married in a span of a couple weeks. Why the rush? I didn't know and I hadn't asked. Lacey was my boss, not my friend. Not to say we weren't friendly. I called her by her first name and we sometimes shared a drink after work, but we'd never be besties. We were just too different.

She was all business.

Which didn't explain her behavior the last few weeks. A quickie wedding to Rock Wolfe was so not Lacey Ward. Er... Lacey Wolfe.

Definitely not. Neither was leaving the firm where she'd gotten her start to take a position with her new husband's company. Her position? Special counsel to the CEO. My position? Executive assistant to special counsel to the CEO.

I loved working with Lacey, and truthfully, I would have followed her just about anywhere.

My generous six-figure salary? Icing on the cake.

Getting away from Blaine Foster? Sugary sprinkles on the icing.

Blaine, a senior partner at the firm, and I had dated a few times. He was old enough to be my father, for sure, but still a sexy silver-haired fox. Problem was, he'd gotten a little too serious with me a little too fast. I wasn't in the market for a permanent relationship, especially not one with a man twice my age who already had grown children. I wanted children of my own...just not quite yet.

I swallowed as I entered the Wolfe Plaza Tower.

Oh. My. God.

If I didn't know better, I'd have thought I was walking into a luxury hotel. Marble tile on the floors, walnut fixtures, and lush paintings on the wall. I'd always been interested in art, in fact had dabbled on my own. I'd considered studying art but had needed to get a marketable skill quickly to pay my bills. My mother couldn't afford college, and my father was busy with *second wife* and *new kids*. I couldn't afford a student loan payment and a career as a starving artist. Six months of paralegal school at a community college, and my fast and accurate fingers had earned me a job as Lacey's assistant.

I strolled through the lobby of the building, eyeing the artwork. One painting in particular drew me in. It was oil on canvas, an abstract, but the darkness of the work immediately made my heart sad.

I wasn't sure why. I couldn't discern any actual images, but the dark reds and blues were twisted together in a corkscrew pattern that almost seemed like a crash into some secret madness.

"Wow," I said out loud.

"What do you think?"

I jerked slightly at the low voice behind me. I turned and held back a gasp. The most beautiful man I'd ever laid eyes on stood a foot away from me, his dark eyes meeting my gaze. He was tall, almost a foot taller than I was. Thank goodness for stilettos. His nearly black hair was long and pulled back into a low ponytail. He wore a crisp designer suit but no tie, the top two buttons of his white cotton shirt undone. Dark stubble graced his jawline.

"Wow," I said again.

"Thank you," he said.

Warmth crept up to my cheeks. He'd asked what I thought of the painting, but I wasn't responding to his query. The "wow" was all him.

"For...what?" I asked.

"For the compliment."

"Oh. You mean...? I didn't mean..."

He chuckled softly. "It's mine."

"What?" My thoughts were a jumble.

"The painting. It's my work."

I lifted my brow. This perfect human was an artist? I looked back at the painting for a signature. I didn't see one, though there was a small symbol at the bottom, like a brand. "It's fascinating."

"It's nice to find someone around here who appreciates art," he said.

"Oh, I definitely do. I paint myself now and then, though I've never created anything so moving."

"Where did you study?" he asked.

Warmth to the cheeks again. "I...didn't. I mean, I didn't go to college."

He let out a soft sound that sounded almost like a scoff. "Most college art programs are overrated. The great ones aren't teaching. They're creating. You're probably better off."

"Hmm. I never looked at it that way."

"What do you see?" he asked me.

"I'm hardly qualified to—"

"You're looking at it. It means something to you. That qualifies you."

I stood silently for a few seconds. How could I discuss this magnificent work of art with the man who painted it?

"Go ahead," he prodded. "I'd really like to know."

"It's...dark yet beautiful. The way the brushstrokes—"

"Forget about the brushstrokes. Forget about the technique. Tell me what you see."

"I see...secrecy."

"And what do you feel?"

"I feel"—I forced my mind to conjure a word that defined the empty feeling—"wistful, I guess."

"You guess?"

"No. Wistful is a good word. Almost sad. And I don't *want* to feel sad, but when I look at it, I can't look away. I'm mesmerized. I keep looking for a key."

"A key to what?"

"I don't mean a literal key. But there's secrecy here. Like something's hiding, and it wants to get out, but..." I shook my head. "I'm probably making no sense at all."

"You're making perfect sense. Go on."

Oh, God. Why had I started this? This man was brilliant, and I sounded like a high school art student trying to impress a teacher. "I can't find any more words. I'm sorry."

"No need to be sorry."

"Did I come anywhere close to what you were going for?" I couldn't help asking.

"It doesn't matter what *I* was going for. What matters is that you like it, that it evoked an emotional response in you. That means I did my job, at least as far as you're concerned."

"As far as *I'm* concerned?"

"Art, as you know, is subjective. What one person loves another might hate."

"No one could hate this," I said.

He smiled. More perfection. I didn't come to work the first day at a new job to have my body react to the first man I met.

But boy, was my body reacting.

"You'd be surprised," he said. "Though I'd rather someone hate it than be indifferent. Hate is still a powerful emotional response."

I stared at him, willing my mouth not to drop open. His words rang so true, yet I'd never considered hate in that way.

I glanced at my watch. Crap. I didn't want to leave this man, but—

"Uh-oh. I'm going to be late. Nice meeting you." I turned and walked—

"There is no key."

His voice. It permeated me as though it had come from within myself.

I looked over my shoulder to catch one more glimpse of the gorgeous artist with more talent in one finger than I'd ever have.

He was already gone.

LACEY STUCK her head into my office. "Settling in?"

"Yeah. I still can't believe I'm working here."

"Believe it." She smiled. "We're all going to be working our butts off until Derek Wolfe's murder is solved."

"It's crazy that all of you are implicated."

"I know. It's ridiculous. I'm finally able to sleep at night, as long as Rock holds me. I know I'm innocent, but how can I prove it when the videotape from my apartment is missing?"

"And the others?"

"All their fingerprints are at the crime scene."

"Why is that even an issue? Especially for Fonda. She was sleeping with Derek, for God's sake. Of course her fingerprints are there."

"They're not leaving any stone unturned, so it's up to us to figure this out."

"Us?"

"Yeah, Charlie. The Wolfes have sources the police don't, and they have a vested interest in proving their innocence. I wouldn't have taken Rock's offer to work here quite so quickly if this other stuff weren't going on."

"But you would have eventually taken it?"

"I don't know. I initially resisted. Corporate law isn't my area, but I'll learn quickly. And to tell you the truth, writing up trusts all day was getting pretty boring. Plus, I'm a Wolfe now. I need to be here to help Rock."

I nodded. "Frankly, Lace, I always thought you were made for bigger and more exciting things than writing wills."

"Yeah, well, corporate stuff will be on the back burner for now. Dealing with the fallout from Derek Wolfe's murder isn't exactly the excitement I banked on. It's becoming downright scary."

A shiver swept over me. I knew what I was getting into by following Lacey over to Wolfe Enterprises. She'd assured me I could stay at the firm and work for another attorney if I wanted to and there would be no hard feelings.

But I'd come along, and not just for the outrageous benefits. I liked working with Lacey, and I wanted to help her clear her name and all the names in her new family. Lacey wasn't a criminal lawyer, and I had no experience in criminal law, but I was willing to learn. I was happy Lacey still wanted me to work for her.

"We'll be in the conference room in fifteen minutes. I need you there to take notes. All the Wolfe brothers will be there."

I'd just arrived, and this was my first day. I had no idea where anything was, how to use the computer system, nothing. But a meeting was a meeting.

"What about the sister?" I asked.

"Riley's still missing." Lacey sighed. "Rock's really worried, and so am I. We'll probably discuss that at the meeting."

"Are you sure you want me there, then? It sounds personal."

"Charlie, until we get all our names cleared, this is part of our business. I need someone I trust there, and I already okayed it with Rock. Be prepared to get very personal with the Wolfes."

I nodded. I could do that. I could do whatever Lacey needed. I owed her a lot. I looked around my new digs. It wasn't a corner executive office, but it was a room instead of a cubicle outside Lacey's office, and it even had a window. I looked out at the early summer day. The rays of the sun shone over the city buildings. I smiled.

This would work out fine.

The boxes I'd packed up at the old office sat in the corner. Might as well at least make this seem like my office. I ripped the tape off one box with a letter opener I found in the top drawer of my desk.

The ding of my phone interrupted my task. A text from Lacey.

We're meeting now. Come to the conference room.

Great. Where the heck was the conference room? I'd need a pad of paper and some pens. Where were they?

No worries. I'd take notes on my phone and figure the paper and pen thing out later. I still had no idea where the conference room was, though.

I raced out of the office, nearly losing my footing as one stiletto heel caught in the short pile carpeting. I held back a *damn*. Probably not a good idea to curse the first day on the job.

I bothered the first person I saw, a young man in a suit. "Excuse me, but this is my first day. Could you tell me where the conference room is?"

"Which one?"

Which one? I had no freaking idea. "The one where Rock Wolfe and his brothers are?"

"Probably their private conference room. Down the hallway to your right. The door should be open if they're expecting you."

"And if it's not?"

"Then enter at your own peril," he said ominously.

Not that he'd freaked me out or anything. I headed down the hall and turned right. The door, thankfully, was open.

I stepped inside and immediately met a dark gaze.

The artist from the lobby sat at one end of the conference table, flanked by his brothers.

Roy Wolfe. Of course. He was an artist, but was usually photographed wearing jeans and a T-shirt, his hair unbound and flowing over his shoulders. I'd seen him once before, at the reading of Derek Wolfe's will. Why that fact hadn't registered this morning in the lobby, I had no idea.

Yeah, I did. I'd been captivated by both him and the painting —so captivated that I was seeing him for the first time.

His lips turned upward ever so slightly.

And my pulse raced.

2

ROY

So the hottie from the lobby was Lacey's assistant. Right, I remembered her now.

Which meant I couldn't pursue her, of course. Not that I would have anyway. I wasn't the pursuing type. My quick one-nighter with a server at a strip club in Montana a little over a week ago had been a fluke. That wasn't me.

"Hey, Charlie," Lacey said. "Everyone, this is my assistant, Charlene Waters. She goes by Charlie."

"Hi," she said timidly.

"Welcome," Rock said. "Don't let these guys overwhelm you. That's Roy next to me and Reid across from me."

Reid and I stood.

"Nice to meet you," Reid said.

I simply nodded.

"Our sister should be here," Rock continued, nodding toward Charlie, "but she's still missing. That's another puzzle we need to solve."

"We won't solve it," Reid said. "Not unless she wants to be found."

Silence for a few deafening seconds.

Then Lacey spoke up. "That's Rock's assistant, Jarrod, and, Reid's assistant, Terrence."

Rock had inherited Jarrod from my father, and Reid had always hired a male assistant. My younger brother was a known womanizer, and my father had taught him to always hire males for positions of trust to avoid any sexual tension and possible claims of harassment. Reid followed the advice, but not because our father had dictated it. He'd actually hired Terrence because he was the best qualified. At least that was what he said. I couldn't care less, frankly.

I didn't have an assistant because I didn't actually work here. This was a meeting to discuss the fallout from our father's murder.

I stayed quiet in these meetings. Right now, though, I was nursing a huge hard-on for the hottie with the light-brown ponytail. She looked adorably uncomfortable in her suit and stilettos. This was a girl who preferred yoga pants and tank tops, I could tell.

Her cheeks were painted a rosy pink that was natural, not the product of makeup. She had a fresh look that I found very inspiring. Most of her features, by themselves, were merely average—average-sized eyes, average nose, average chin, average light-brown hair. But her fine bone structure took all those average parts and put them together in a uniquely beautiful way, drawing attention to the silvery radiance of her irises. I could make her image come alive on canvas. Show the world what true beauty was, for she shined beauty not just from the outside, but from the inside as well. Through her appreciation of the finer things in life.

She appreciated art, and by only knowing that about her, I already knew so much.

She probably appreciated music, gourmet food, fine wine…

I wanted to know.

I wanted to get inside her head and find out everything about Miss Charlene Waters.

Shit. She *was* a "miss," wasn't she? Luckily, she was holding her phone and typing into it as Lacey spoke, so I discreetly checked out her left hand. No wedding ring.

Thank God.

Not that I was interested.

Except that I was.

I was so bad with women, and getting involved with someone who worked for the company wasn't the smartest path.

But damn. I wanted this woman. Right here. Right now. If I could grab her and fuck her right on the oblong conference room table, I would.

How to approach her?

Easy. She admired my work. She liked art. I could take her to the Met. Of course, an art lover like her had probably been there numerous times. I could take her to one of my showings. Or I could take her to my private studio and show her what I was currently working on. Afterward, we could have some wine and cheese at a small tavern.

I held back a scoff. To do any of this, I'd have to ask her.

That was the part I sucked at.

Sure, it was fine to talk to a stranger in the lobby about one of my paintings.

But a woman I was interested in?

That didn't come easy to me.

Not that any of this mattered.

It couldn't happen for one important reason.

My own mind prevented me from getting involved with anyone seriously. I was a mess, for I held a secret darker and more hidden than anything my painting showed to the most noted art connoisseur. A secret trapped in my subconscious.

And the key she'd been looking for?

It didn't exist.

3

CHARLIE

I forced myself to type rapidly into my phone. If only I'd brought my tablet today. Lacey said the company would supply one but I hadn't gotten it yet. My skin was icy and my pulse in overdrive just from the nearness of Roy Wolfe.

No. Must concentrate.

Failing to document even a few seconds of this important discussion wouldn't bode well for my first day on the job.

I typed furiously, capturing every detail. The information went in and out of my head so quickly I barely knew what I was typing. I stayed quiet. My job here was to be the conduit of information.

"Charlie?"

I nearly typed "Charlie" before I realized Lacey was addressing me.

I looked up. "Yeah?"

"Could you go down to the lobby? Our lunch is on the way, but they won't come up here."

Not even for the Wolfes? Surprising. "Yeah. Sure." Lunchtime already? We'd started at ten. Had I truly been taking notes for two hours? I rose.

"I'll go with her." Jarrod stood. "She may need help carrying everything."

"Good idea," Rock said. "Thanks, Jarrod."

"No problem."

"Crap," Rock continued. "Wait. I need you for something else. Terrence, can you go?"

Roy stood then. "I'll go."

My body erupted in quivers. I tamped them down as well as I could.

"Okay, that'll work," Reid said. "We're officially on our lunch-break. No business until Roy and Charlie get back."

"You mean no business until after lunch," Rock said. "You're not dragging me into your 'I'm too busy to take time off to eat' thing."

"That's why we order in, Rock," Reid said. "So we can continue working."

"Well, fuck that." Rock loosened his tie. "We'll go out, then."

"The food has already been ordered," Lacey reminded him. "That's why Charlie and Roy are going downstairs."

"We're still taking a solid hour for lunch." Rock eyed Reid. "You need to learn how to take some time for yourself, bro."

I stood there, mesmerized by the dynamic. Rock, the reluctant CEO, a biker from Montana in the position only because his dead father's will mandated it. Reid, the youngest brother who'd been groomed to take over but relegated to second fiddle.

And behind me, the middle brother. Roy Wolfe. Quiet. Creative. A reclusive genius. An old soul.

Nothing like either of his brothers.

A truly magnificent work of art in himself. The gods had definitely smiled on him when he was born.

"They'll be arguing about this for a while," Roy said quietly. "Let's go."

We left the conference room and Roy closed the door behind us.

Silence as we walked to the elevator.

Silence as Roy pressed L for lobby.

Silence as we descended. Roy seemed...rigid.

Silence when the door opened, and we walked across the tiled floor.

The thought-provoking painting again drew my gaze, and I slowed my pace. Then I turned to Roy. "Why didn't you tell me who you were?"

"Because I wanted you to see me as the artist, not as Roy Wolfe."

"I don't even know Roy Wolfe. Why would it have mattered?"

"Because I wanted your honest opinion. Not the opinion you'd give an heir to the Wolfe fortune."

"What makes you think I wouldn't have been honest?"

He chuckled. "No one wants to criticize a Wolfe, silver."

Silver? "Uh...what?"

"You heard me."

"My name's Charlie."

"I know that."

"Then why did you call me silver?"

"Your eyes. They're silver. Sparkling silver. I've never seen eyes like yours."

Wow. Double Wow. My eyes were gray, maybe a hint of blue. Honestly, my most mundane feature. Sparkling silver? Not even close.

"I'd like to paint those eyes," he continued.

Wow again.

I opened my mouth, but nothing came out.

"Looks like lunch is here." Roy strode toward a young guy carrying two bags with a nearby Indian restaurant logo on them.

For a few seconds, I stood dumbly, unable to make my feet

follow him. I simply gaped at him, his suit fitting so perfectly on his body, his nearly black hair hanging in a silky tail over the dark gray wool.

He took the two bags, mumbled some words to the delivery guy, and then he turned back to me.

"I guess I could've handled this myself," I said.

"These are actually pretty heavy," he said. "I got them."

"Then you don't need me."

"You got plans or something?"

"Well...no." Could I be any more stupid? "I mean, just lunch upstairs with the rest of you."

He laughed softly. "That's what I thought."

A tiny sliver of anger poked at me. He was making fun of me. I walked silently behind him as we headed toward the elevators. Roy's hands were full, so I pressed the button. Again, silence as we rode up to the fiftieth floor. I'd learned this morning that the forty-ninth and fiftieth floors were the main offices of Wolfe Enterprises. The fifty-first and fifty-second were the Wolfe family residences. Rock's penthouse on floor fifty-two was still roped off by the police.

My body was hyperaware of the man standing next to me. I'd never had sex in an elevator, and oh my God, right now would be a perfect time to remedy that. Roy Wolfe in an elevator? Already I was getting wet thinking about it.

But Roy Wolfe was silent, staring at the elevator doors, probably wishing they'd open so we could get out of this awkward silence.

I breathed a sigh of relief when the bell dinged, indicating we'd reached our floor. The doors began to glide open—

Roy set the two bags of food on the floor of the elevator and quickly pushed the "doors close" button. He turned to me, his dark gaze unreadable.

"Will you have dinner with me tonight?" he asked.

My mouth dropped open.

"Please, silver?"

Please? Hell, he didn't have to say please. Still, he was a Wolfe, and I worked for the company. "Are you sure that's...appropriate?"

"Appropriate? You do eat, don't you?" His eyes were still unreadable. Gorgeous and long-lashed, but still unreadable.

I squinted slightly, trying—and failing—to analyze his enigmatic expression. "Well...yeah. I mean, I work for you."

"You work for Lacey."

"I work for the company. *Your* company."

"I'm not a part of the company, silver. Rock and Reid run it— Rock under duress, I might add. I'm a silent partner if there ever was one."

"Still..."

"Never mind." He pushed the "door open" button. "I get it." He walked out of the elevator carrying the bags.

Good job, Charlie. You just let the most interesting man you ever met walk out of your life. He calls you silver, for God's sake. Silver!

What a moron I was.

I followed Roy numbly back to the conference room. As Roy suspected, Reid and Rock were still arguing over whether they'd continue working through lunch.

"Don't make me play the CEO card," Rock said.

Reid rolled his eyes. "CEO in name only. That's what you like to tell me. Until it suits your purpose."

"Hell, yeah. And right now it suits my purpose. We're not working through lunch." He directed Jarrod, Terrence, and me to get the food set out while the rest of them cleared their work stuff off the table.

Jarrod and Terrence were great, and I liked them both immediately. The two of them were actually best friends, a bromance if I ever saw one, though physically they couldn't have been more different. Jarrod was tall, dark-skinned, and rugged sexy with short dreadlocks, and Terrence was shorter but more buff, fair-skinned, and sported a shaved head. Both were incredibly good-looking.

Of course neither was as magnificent as Roy Wolfe, who was now refusing to meet my gaze.

"You're not taking this seriously, Rock," Reid said.

"Because I'd like to take a break to eat? For fuck's sake."

Terrence chuckled under his breath, nearly making me break into nervous giggles. We quickly got the food set out.

Once we'd all filled plates and returned to our seats, the room became eerily quiet.

"See?" Reid took a drink from his bottle of water. "We should be working."

"What? We must have conversation during lunch or we have to work?" Rock shook his head. "You've gone off the deep end. Enjoy your food, everyone. Don't talk if you don't feel like it."

This first lunch on the job turned out to be the longest meal I'd ever sat through. Or so it seemed, at least. I had to force myself not to look at Roy, though it wouldn't have mattered if I had. He was still refusing to meet my gaze.

I'd made a huge mistake, though I truly *was* concerned about the appropriateness of going out with one of the Wolfes when I worked for the company. This was my first day. My first day!

As soon as we were done here, I'd grab Lacey and get her input.

I swallowed a bit of the tikka masala, normally a favorite of mine. It tasted like dirt.

Whether Lacey put my mind at ease no longer mattered.

I'd blown what might have been the best thing to happen to me ever.

4

ROY

I'd fucked up again.

There was a reason I didn't do this. A reason other than the mindfuck I lived with constantly. I was attracted to Charlie Waters. More attracted than I'd been to a woman in a long time. Enough to let go of the mindfuck for a minute and take a chance.

And still I'd failed. Just because I'd had a hot one-nighter with a server in Montana clearly didn't mean I'd magically transformed into a man who swept women off their feet.

I'd made a fool of myself.

Yeah. Back to having no luck with women. Great.

I kept my eyes off Charlie. If I looked her way, I wouldn't be able to drag my gaze away. I'd never get her image out of my mind as it was. Until the day I died, those silver eyes would haunt me.

I ate, but not because I was hungry. I'd lost my appetite. I ate to save face. Stupid, but true. I ached to get out of this conference room, out of this building, out of...

Maybe I should pull a Riley and just disappear. My little sister was notorious for her escape routine. No one knew what would push her over the edge, but something would eventually.

She'd be back. She always came back.

Still, I worried about her while she was gone. We all did. She and I weren't overly close. I wasn't overly close to my brothers either.

I wasn't overly close to anyone.

I preferred being alone. Not that I didn't like a good fuck as much as the next guy. I just wasn't sure a relationship was in the cards for me. The Montana fling would have to hold me for a while. I was the worst at picking up women, and I refused to join an internet dating site.

No way. Just no way.

I also refused to pay for sex, even though I could afford the best out there.

No way. Just no way.

Since little miss silver eyes wasn't interested, I'd go it solo, as usual. I'd gone way out of my comfort zone to ask her to dinner, and I'd gotten shot down.

I work for the company. Your company.

What a dumbass excuse. What she really meant was *I'm not interested.*

Normally this wouldn't be a huge issue. I'd just stay away from the office. Not an option at the moment, though. Until we figured out how and why all our prints ended up in our father's penthouse that night, I needed to be involved. All of our lives were at stake here, even though I had no doubt that every single one of us was innocent. Rock hadn't even been in New York that night.

Yet all of our prints had been found at the murder site.

I'd been at my loft all night.

Alone.

I was always alone.

Almost always, anyway, so the fact that I had no witnesses shouldn't be a surprise to anyone. I had to find a way to clear myself, which meant it was a good thing I'd chickened out on confiding in Rock.

If he—or anyone—knew what I knew—what I kept so deeply buried—I'd be fucked. Really fucked.

NINE O'CLOCK, and I'd just settled in for a night of painting. My brothers kept me at the damned office until nearly seven. Or rather, that was when I told them I was leaving. Another minute of avoiding that silver-eyed gaze would have driven me mad.

Mad with lust, that is.

The most ridiculous thing about the day was that nothing had been accomplished. Nine hours of discussion and strategizing, and we were no closer to proving any of our innocence. We'd been questioned ad nauseum, but so far not one of us had been arrested. The cops were apparently strategizing as well. We weren't yet considered suspects, other than Lacey. The rest of us were merely "persons of interest." Reid and Rock both maintained that we needed to stay one step ahead of the police. If we didn't, we'd all fall.

I agreed with them in theory. In practice? I wasn't sure. Yeah, we had the money to hire the best people, but we weren't our father. We wouldn't use our money to "get rid" of damning evidence.

At least *I* wouldn't.

I barely knew Rock.

But Reid had been under the tutelage of our father.

Our father had been a bad man.

A very bad man.

I knew something my siblings didn't, something that needed

to stay embedded in my mind forever. I couldn't even let myself think about it, for fear it would come out. I'd buried it so deep, I wasn't even sure what it was anymore. All I knew was that it had to stay fossilized in the rock of my brain.

Or my life would be over.

I began mixing oil paints on my palette, when—

I jumped.

My intercom had buzzed.

Strange.

My intercom never buzzed except on the rare occasions I had food delivered at odd hours. I usually went out to eat or fixed a sandwich at home.

I clicked the button. "Yeah?"

"Hi."

The voice was familiar. My groin tightened. "Who is it?" Though I knew.

"Charlie Waters. May I...come up?"

"What for?"

A sigh. "Never mind. This was a mistake."

Let her go, man. Just let her go.

Yeah, right.

"You can come up." I pressed the button to open the main door.

The loft was a mess. I wasn't the best housekeeper in the world, and I didn't let anyone come in to clean. I was afraid they'd mess up my supplies. I was wearing old jeans and a T-shirt with my painting smock over it. My hair was up in a messy man bun.

Fuck. No time. This was me. The artist. She'd have to take me as I was.

A minute later, she knocked softly. I quickly put down my palette and walked to the door.

She stood, still in her work clothes, looking worn and tired but still delectable.

"Hi," she said meekly.

I held the door open. "Come in."

She stepped in slowly, saying nothing.

I said nothing.

When I finally decided to speak, she spoke at the same time.

"Go ahead," she said.

"No, you go ahead. You came *here*, remember?"

"Yeah." A pink blush crept into her cheeks. "I wanted to apologize."

"For what? If you didn't want to have dinner with me, there's no need to apologize."

She squeezed her hands into fists. "You've twisted everything around."

"How?"

"I was worried. I just started a new job today at your company."

"I told you, it's not my com—"

Her silver eyes sparkled with fire. "That's bullshit and you know it. It's Wolfe Enterprises. You're a Wolfe."

I stayed silent.

What could I say to that? As many times as I'd wanted to renounce my birthright, I was indeed a Wolfe.

"I talked to Lacey."

"About what?"

"Um...about whether having dinner with you was an issue. She said she didn't think it would be a problem, so..."

"So what? You're here to accept the invitation I made hours ago? Sorry. It's been rescinded."

Asshole move, totally. I regretted the words as soon as they left my mouth. I wasn't an asshole. Either of my brothers might have made that move. Not me.

"Oh." She looked away. "I guess I should go, then."

"I suppose." Another asshole move. What the hell was wrong with me?

"I'm sorry I bothered you." She turned and walked out the door.

Was I really going to let that beautiful woman with silver eyes walk out of my loft?

Out of my life?

"Wait a minute, silver," I said.

She turned, her eyes wide. "What?"

"The invitation was rescinded because it's nine o'clock. I've already had dinner."

"Oh." Her eyes brightened. "Maybe another time, then."

"You mean you haven't eaten?"

She shook her head. "I just left the office."

"They didn't buy you dinner for staying late?"

"They didn't know I stayed. I wanted to unpack my personals and learn where everything is."

"You're a workaholic like the rest of them, huh?"

She let out an adorable little huff. "I believe in doing the best job I can at all times, if that's what you mean."

"That's something we share, then."

"I don't mean to change the subject," she said, "but you really are a brilliant artist."

Warmth crept through me. I'd had my share of compliments from those in the cultural elite, but this endorsement from a woman I hardly knew suddenly became the most important review I'd ever received.

She looked around the mess in my living room. "You don't have any of your work on your walls."

"No."

"Why?"

"There are plenty of unfinished works in my studio." I pointed down the small hallway.

"But why not in here? For visitors to enjoy?"

"Visitors?" I never had visitors. Even on the few occasions I'd gotten lucky, we'd always gone to her place except once.

"Yeah. You know. People who come over to see you." She laughed teasingly.

"No one comes to see me," I said truthfully.

"Well...*I'm* here."

"You're the first." Maybe not the first, but close. "How did you know where I live, anyway?"

"I have access to all the personnel files at the company now. It wasn't difficult to find your address."

"Oh." I felt oddly exposed. She was Lacey's assistant, so this made perfect sense. Jarrod and Terrence had the same access. No one else, other than my brothers, did.

"And you changed the subject. Why don't you have your work on the walls?"

"None of it fits." A simple explanation that wasn't even close to the truth. All of my work was so personal, and although I displayed it in galleries and in the Wolfe building, and though a lot of it hung in strangers' homes, I never felt right displaying it in my own. I painted for myself, but still... If I couldn't explain it to myself, I certainly couldn't explain it to Charlie.

"Of course it would fit. You're the artist."

"Where would you like to go to dinner?"

"You're changing the subject."

"You're the one who showed up here begging for a dinner invitation." Man. Asshole move again. What the hell was wrong with me?

"You're right." She lowered her gaze. "I'm sorry. I'll get out of your way."

I was the worst with women! Here was someone who had

piqued my interest, who had eyes I'd never forget, and I couldn't stop being a douche.

She turned to leave, but I grabbed her arm.

"Wait."

Her silver eyes met mine. She looked...bereft.

"I'm sorry. Please. I want to have dinner with you. Tomorrow?"

"Are you going to rescind the invitation?" she asked, her tone hurt.

"No. Not if you accept it."

"All right. I accept." She pulled a card out of her purse. "My work extension is on here. Call me with the details."

"I'd rather call your cell."

"Why?"

"Because I don't want to call the company. That was the issue you had in the beginning, remember?"

"Well, okay. I guess." She grabbed a pen out of her bag, scribbled some numbers on the card, and then handed it to me. "I always have my cell on me. Except for when I don't."

I chuckled. "What exactly does that mean?"

"It means sometimes I forget my phone. But not usually."

This woman was precious! She was beautifully flustered, and her hair was in disarray. The look in her eyes—I couldn't even describe it.

But I knew one thing.

I wanted to paint it—paint *her*—right now, with that look.

5

CHARLIE

He grabbed my hand, not gently, and stared deep into my eyes. His dark eyes were burning, and I swore they melted me into a puddle of butter right in his entryway.

"Don't go," he said simply.

I opened my mouth but had no idea what to say. I hadn't eaten. Did he want to have dinner? Or did he want to...

I had the feeling that Roy Wolfe wasn't either of his brothers. Reid was a known womanizer, and Rock... Well, Lacey hadn't confided in me about their first encounter in her office, but I had ears. They hadn't exactly been quiet. I was thankful no one else had walked by during their little interlude. Her partnership at the firm could have been jeopardized.

Didn't matter now. She no longer worked there.

"Are you going to say anything?" he asked.

"I...have work in the morning." God, what an idiot! This was far from my first encounter with a handsome man, but I was acting like a shy schoolgirl who just got asked out by the football captain.

"I know. I wasn't asking you to spend the night."

Warmth crept up my neck and into my cheeks. "Of course not. I knew that. So...dinner?"

"If you want. I'll order something for you. You don't want to be thinking about food while you're posing."

My heart fluttered. "Posing?"

"Yeah. In fact, I'm sorry, but dinner will have to wait. I promise you a gourmet feast if you let me paint you right now, with that faraway look in your eyes. I've just got to capture that on canvas."

"Posing?" I echoed, sounding like a complete imbecile.

"Yeah. Please. I've got to paint you, and it has to be now."

My heart thundered so loud I thought he might be able to hear it. He wanted to paint *me*? Charlie Waters? Plain Jane? My appetite no longer seemed important. This man—this extraordinary artist—wanted me to be his next subject.

Me.

Me.

"Sure. I guess so."

"No 'I guess so.' Yes. Be absolutely sure. We both need to be all in."

His dark eyes were burning with fire. Passion. For me.

But not for me, really. For something I represented. Something he wanted to immortalize on canvas.

It was a start.

"Yes. Yes, Roy," I said, trying to sound confident. "I will pose for you."

"Thank God. Follow me." He led me through the living area. A small kitchen sat on the other side, and then a short hallway where two doors stood. One was open. The studio. I inhaled, expecting to smell the piney resin scent of turpentine or mineral spirits.

Hmm. Nothing.

The other door was his bedroom. It had to be.

He raked his gaze over me. "I wish it were daylight. I could capture you so much better in natural light, but this will have to do. You'll have to change."

"Change? You wanted to paint me as I am."

He smiled. "I mean change clothes. That crisp suit is too businesslike. I want to see you as you truly are."

"You mean...naked?"

"I was going to give you a robe, but if you're offering..."

"I'm not," I said quickly, though the thought had merit. If I got naked...

No. This man was an artist. He'd asked me to dinner, but that didn't mean he wanted to take me to bed.

He opened a closet. This was obviously another bedroom that he used for a studio. "I don't paint here often. I have a studio a couple buildings over where I have more room to move around."

"I don't smell any paint," I said.

"Contrary to popular belief, oil paints have no odor. You're probably thinking of turpentine or other solvents. I use a different method to clean my brushes."

"How?"

"Raw linseed oil." He smiled. "Doubles as a nutritional supplement too."

"What?"

"Linseed oil is another term for flaxseed oil."

"I didn't know that. My mother takes flaxseed for her cholesterol."

Roy nodded. "It has a nutty smell, much better than the noxious odor of turpentine or mineral spirits. A little of the oil will remove the color from the brushes and help keep the bristles from becoming dry. That plus a little castile soap and water does the trick."

"Oh."

"Plus, it's summer, so I can have the windows open, which creates a nice cross breeze if the nutty odor bothers you."

"It doesn't. I actually don't smell anything."

"This is the master suite, but I sleep in the other room. I need the space here for supplies and—" He pulled out a plush white robe and handed it to me. "Here."

I took it from him, my hands sinking into the silky chenille. "Where should I change?"

"You can use the bedroom."

I warmed all over. Roy Wolfe's bedroom. What might it look like? He wasn't the rugged mountain-man type like Rock, or the sleek businessman type like Reid.

Roy Wolfe was a combination of both, plus something more special.

His bedroom was a mystery to me, one I'd solve as soon as I opened the door and entered.

"All right," I said finally. "The closed door?"

"Yeah."

"Okay. Be right back."

I walked out, trying not to go too quickly, even though curiosity about Roy's bedroom was killing me. When I opened the door to the other room, I dropped my mouth open.

It was nothing like I expected. The thickest mattress I'd ever seen sat on a black steel bedframe that could have come from IKEA. The bed was covered in plain white sheets and a chocolate brown comforter. Against the other wall was an antique highboy and chest, made out of walnut was my best guess. IKEA and antiques. Roy's decorating style was truly eclectic, which was strange, given his artistic talent.

But he showed that in abundance on the other wall facing the window. He'd painted—or I assumed he'd painted—an abstract of the New York City skyline, complete with ghostly images of the Twin Towers that had collapsed years ago. A soft cloud of light swirled above them, seeming to encase them. I sucked in a breath. I had no words. It was truly stunning. Roy wouldn't display his work in his home where others could see it, but here, in his bedroom—his sanctuary—he'd created a masterpiece.

A small door led to an attached bathroom with a clawed tub and separate shower. The bathroom seemed small, until I remembered that this wasn't the master suite, which would have a decadent bathroom.

Another door housed what I assumed was a closet. I fought the urge to open it. I was already invading his privacy.

No. Just change, Charlie, and get out of here, back to Roy.

I shed my work clothes but left my bra and panties on. Then I wrapped the luxurious robe around me, my nipples hard against the lace of my bra. I itched to touch myself, to pinch my nipples and feel the ripple of pleasure it would bring.

I closed my eyes and imagined Roy's firm lips encircling one, his fingers tugging at the other. I squirmed against the tickle between my legs.

He just wants to paint you, Charlie. You're getting overeager.

Of course, he also asked you to dinner...

I stopped the jabbering in my brain, adjusted the band holding my ponytail—half the hair had come out of it. What must I have looked like when I showed up at his door?—and walked back to the studio. The door was still open, so I walked in casually. At least I hoped I looked casual. Inside, my heart was beating a mile a minute.

Roy had his head bent over a palette, mixing paint.

I cleared my throat in what I hoped was a ladylike manner.

He looked up and studied me. No smile, but he regarded me intently.

"Can you take your hair down?" he asked.

"Yeah. Sure." I pulled the scrunchie and then shook my head to let the hair fall sort of into place. "Let me go brush it out."

"No. Don't. It's perfect just the way it is."

"It's got to be a mess."

"It is. I like it. It goes great with that faraway sparkle in your eyes. Just what I'm going for."

Faraway sparkle? Horny sparkle was more like it. I knew well what my hair looked like after I took it out of a ponytail.

A mess.

A big mess.

Hardly what went with any kind of sparkle.

"Really, it will look better if I just brush it out."

"I won't hear of it. Come here and sit on this stool." He gestured. "I'll need to adjust the lighting."

I obeyed and sat down, letting the robe open to show a fair amount of cleavage. This wasn't like me, but I wanted Roy to look at me. To really look at my body, which was pretty darned good. Thank you, yoga and Jazzercize.

He didn't seem to notice the exposed chest, though. He busied himself with the lighting, and then he touched my hair and rearranged it a little.

Hair had no feeling, but I swore electricity shot through his fingertips into my scalp and throughout my whole body. The tickle between my legs intensified.

"Beautiful," he murmured, meeting my gaze.

His eyes seemed almost black, as if they'd darkened, which I didn't think was possible. Must have been my imagination.

"Th-Thank you."

"Your eyes... I know I've said this before, but I've never seen anything like them, silver. They're the color of the full moon shining through a night fog."

I couldn't stop a squeaky sigh from coming out of my throat.

His words did more for my body and my mind than Blaine Foster, or anyone else, ever had.

He gazed at me intently. "You ready?"

"S-Sure."

"I'm going to put my interpretation of you on this canvas, but know this, silver. It will never be as beautiful as you are."

That damned squeaky sigh again...accompanied by a growl from my stomach, a reminder that I hadn't eaten since the lunch in the conference room—the lunch Roy and I had picked up in the lobby, the lunch he set down when he asked me to dinner, the lunch where he refused to meet my gaze.

He didn't appear to have heard my stomach's hungry protest. Good. Here I was, modeling for a professional artist, and I couldn't keep my body from making inappropriate noises. If I got gassy, I'd be mortified.

"Keep your back straight," he said, regarding his canvas.

Had I been slouching? I corrected my posture. The stool had no back, so I had to make myself sit up straight.

"Good," he said, without looking.

"How do you know I did anything?"

"I heard the robe rustle. As an artist, I've trained all of my senses to be a little more aware."

"Why don't you let your models sit in a chair with a back?"

"Because I want to see you as you are, not propped up by something inanimate."

"Okay." I wasn't sure I understood, but I wanted to do whatever I could to make this easy for him. If he enjoyed painting me, he might ask to do it again, and then I'd get to see him once more.

Of course he'd already asked me to dinner. In fact, he'd promised me a gourmet feast if I posed for him. My stomach gurgled again.

His shoulders quivered slightly. Shit. He'd heard! Of course he'd heard. He just got done telling me how great his senses were. No reason to get upset. We were adults here, and all adults knew that stomachs growled when they were hungry.

"How long will this take?"

"I'll get the nuances down in an hour or so. Then you can eat."

"No worries. Take as long as you need."

"I don't want to keep you past midnight. I know you have work tomorrow."

"Yeah. True."

"Now we need to stop talking. I want you to look at the wall, focus on the spot right over my head, okay?"

I nodded. At least I wouldn't be looking right at him. That helped. Otherwise I'd need to squirm against the pressure between my legs.

I might need to anyway.

Roy Wolfe was the sexiest man I'd ever met. Truly.

He washed the canvas in a gray. First I thought it was black, but then I realized the color on his brush wasn't complete darkness.

"You don't have to let the background dry?" I asked.

"Nope. Not with the technique I plan to use. Now no more talking."

"Right. Sorry."

Focusing on the wall above his shoulder, I could only see him peripherally, and I longed to watch the expression on his face as he brushed my image onto his canvas.

I remained as still as I could, with the throbbing between my legs.

6

ROY

The dark gray represented nighttime. Her moonlit features would be more pronounced against darkness. Her caramel-colored hair fell in sporadic loose waves around her shoulders. If only she'd shed the robe, and I could see her in her naked glory.

But it was too soon for that. I was too attracted to her. She wasn't just any model. She was a woman I wanted in my bed. *Really* wanted in my bed. If I saw her body, I wouldn't be able to capture what I longed to on this canvas.

The lighting cast silver highlights in her hair, and I brushed little glints of zinc white over the soft browns.

The flesh tones of her face were easy to paint and contour. First things first, because what I wanted to focus on were those eyes.

So silvery and sparkling, they gazed above my shoulders as I'd instructed her. Good thing. If she were looking *at* me, I wouldn't be able to concentrate. As it was, I was having a hard time, but I placed my need to paint her above the ache in my groin.

I mixed the zinc white with a touch of ivory black and added some blues. Nope. I tried again. Nope. Then once more. A little closer.

I began painting her eyes. Damn. Still not perfect. Why was that silvery hue eluding me?

"Fuck," I said aloud.

"What's wrong?"

"It's your eyes. They're not right."

"How long has it been?" she asked.

It had probably seemed like hours to her. I knew well how difficult modeling was. I'd done it during college. "A little less than an hour."

"How much do you have done?"

"Everything. Except the eyes aren't right."

"You painted a whole portrait in an hour?"

"It's an abstract, and yeah. But I'm not happy with—"

She hopped off the stool. "Let me see."

I opened my mouth to try to stop her, but she moved quickly. She faced the canvas with wide eyes.

"Wow. Just wow."

"It's not right. The eyes."

"How can you say that? This is more beautiful than I ever imagined."

I gazed into her eyes. "No, it's not. Not as beautiful as you are."

"But it *is*. You made my hair so...so... And my eyes... It doesn't look like me at all. I mean, it does, but... It looks like the best version of me, you know what I mean?"

"I do."

But it didn't. It didn't capture her ethereal essence. That silveriness in her eyes existed only in her. No pigment could replicate it, even with a master mixing it.

"I can't believe it. You're so gifted, Roy. So much talent."

"It's not my best work."

"It is to me."

Her pink lips were parted and shiny. I couldn't help myself. I set down my palette, grabbed her, and pulled her to me. For a few precious seconds, I stared at the miracle that was her, thinking I couldn't touch her, just couldn't, because it might mar her perfection.

Then her tongue touched her bottom lip, and I couldn't help myself. I crushed my lips to hers.

Her mouth was already open, so I pushed my tongue in. She tasted like crisp apple wine. A soft moan hummed from her throat into my mouth, and I deepened the kiss, holding her tightly.

My smock was covered in oil paints. I'd ruin this robe, but I didn't care. I was a Wolfe. I could buy a million robes. Even if I couldn't, this kiss was well worth it.

The inside of her mouth felt like smooth silk. Her arms crept around my neck, the touch of her soft fingers making me even hotter. My cock was already pounding against my jeans, demanding release.

I wanted her. I wanted Charlie Waters in my bed, and I wanted her there now.

I'd promised to feed her. Her tummy growling had been so cute.

But damn, she was kissing me back. Kissing me with urgency, all the urgency I felt myself. I cupped one of her cheeks and then trailed back to her head, threading my fingers through her disheveled hair. So soft, like blades of wheat grass on a summer day.

Again, the paint. Surely I was painting her. Didn't care. Didn't fucking care at all.

With my other hand, I untied the robe and swept it off her shoulder, letting it hang on one side of her. Then I cupped her pert breast still encased in her bra. Her nipple was hard against the fabric, and I thumbed it gently.

She shuddered against me, groaning into my mouth.

Good. She liked that. I liked it too.

I wanted that hard little nipple in my mouth, between my teeth. I wanted to nip at it until she was squirming like crazy.

I moved my other hand downward, shoving the soiled robe off her other shoulder. It fell into a heap on the floor. Our mouths were still fused together, so I couldn't see, but if she was still wearing a bra, she was no doubt still wearing panties as well.

Damn. My cock was throbbing.

I'd just had sex recently with a waitress in Montana, and already I was way more turned on after one kiss with Charlie Waters.

I broke the kiss with a loud smack, panting. "I want you, Charlie," I said huskily.

"I"—*inhale*—"want you too."

"Fuck." I unclasped her bra quickly and freed her breasts. God, they were more amazing than I'd imagined. Pert and perky, medium-sized and perfect, fair with reddish-brown nipples that were hardened into little knobs.

I was going to take her. I was going to take her right here in my studio. My studio was my haven. I'd never done anything other than paint in here.

That was changing tonight.

I eased her panties down her hips until they met the floor. Then I unsnapped my jeans and freed my aching erection. I lifted her, still wearing my soiled smock, and set her down on my hard cock.

"Condom?" she said on a breath.

Shit. Really? I was usually so careful. "Clean. You?"

"Yeah. And on the pill. Thank God." She sighed. "Feels so good."

God, did it. She was wet for me. So wet, and sans condom I could feel every ridge inside her.

I hadn't kissed her body. I hadn't touched her smooth folds. I hadn't sucked on those amazing nipples.

Hell, I hadn't even undressed.

I'd never in my life been so hungry for a woman that I neglected to undress.

But here I was, holding this beautiful naked woman in my arms, fucking her against a wall in my studio.

"Roy, oh my God!" She clamped around me, milking me with her climax.

This wouldn't take long.

Not long at all.

"Ah! God!" I released inside her, filling her.

And feeling more alive than I had in a long time.

7

CHARLIE

When he stopped pulsating, Roy eased me off his cock until my feet touched the floor. Sweat from his brow dripped onto me and slid down the side of my face in a tiny warm river.

Then he looked at me with a searing gaze. "That's not how I wanted this to go."

Was he regretting it already? I wasn't sure what to say.

He cleared his throat. "I mean, look at you. Gray and brown paint all over your beautiful body from my smock."

I hadn't noticed until he mentioned it. Sure enough, oil pigments were smudged all over my chest, abdomen, and thighs.

"It's okay."

"You don't understand. I wanted to have you in a bed, where we could go slowly, where I could gaze into those eyes..."

Though my heart had finally slowed down after the fucking, it now sped up again with full force.

Silence for what seemed like a long time, until my tummy growled again.

That got a little smile out of him. "I promised you food."

"It's late," I said. "Don't worry about it."

"Nope. I promised, and I always keep a promise. I'll order something. What do you like?"

"Everything. From chateaubriand to pizza. I like everything."

"How about Thai? There's a great place that delivers quickly."

"Will they deliver this late?"

"Yup. I don't exactly keep normal hours. When inspiration strikes, I paint, and meals wait until I can take a break. I'll call them. In the meantime, you can use my bathroom to take a shower if you want."

Did he know he was being a little dismissive? He hadn't even asked me what I wanted from the Thai place. Of course, I'd said I ate everything. As long as it didn't contain goat cheese—not exactly a Thai staple—I'd be good. "All right."

"There's some grapeseed oil on the bathroom counter. It will help get the oil color off you if you have trouble."

"Oh." I hadn't thought of that. Then again, I'd never been covered in oil paint. I held up the robe. "This is ruined, I think. I'm sorry."

"So what? I'll get more." He smiled.

And my heart started pounding all over again. He was surely the most beautiful man in the world. Why wasn't he a model like his sister? He was perfect.

"Uh...okay. I guess I'll take a shower, then."

I walked out of the studio, back to his bedroom, and into the bathroom. I closed the door behind me and—

"Oh my God." My reflection stared at me. My hair was in complete disarray, and yes, my body was smudged all over with oil paint, mostly shades of silvery gray. He truly had been trying to get my eyes exactly right.

I stared at my eyes in the mirror.

Blue-gray eyes, a little too small, nothing special. While not my worst feature, they were far from my best.

But Roy Wolfe saw something in them, something I couldn't define.

Silver? I laughed quietly as I shook my head. They weren't silver.

Silver was the color of the moon shining on snow-covered pine trees.

My eyes were dull gray.

I turned on the shower and waited until it began to steam up the mirror, covering the "silver" of my eyes. I dabbed some of the grapeseed oil on my body and then stepped under the warm pelting water.

Perfect. It felt perfect. I used the shampoo and body wash to thoroughly cleanse myself, and then I stepped out and turned off the water.

I wrapped a large bath towel around my body and looked again in the mirror. Something felt different, but I wasn't sure what.

Then I realized. It was my skin. My skin felt...nice. Nice and moisturized. Usually I felt tight and itchy until I applied lotion all over my body.

What was different?

My gaze fell on the bottle of grapeseed oil. It had removed the paint and also left me feeling like I was on a tropical island. I smiled at myself.

This was turning out to be a great night.

I dried off and realized I hadn't brought my clothes in with me. I toweled off my hair, wrapped another dry towel around my chest, and walked out to the bedroom to get my clothes.

Roy stood in the bedroom, holding a clean robe and smiling. "Here."

"Thanks." I walked back into the bathroom to put the robe on and laughed aloud. He'd just seen me naked. Why was I suddenly so modest?

I shed the towel and wrapped myself in the robe and went back out. The mural met my gaze. "Tell me about this." I nodded toward it.

"Just something I threw together."

"Just something you threw together? You're kidding, right?'"

"Not really. I couldn't sleep one night, so I got up, and this is the result."

"It's amazing, but you said you didn't display your work here."

"This is my bedroom. It's hardly on display."

"You mean you don't... Never mind."

"What?"

"Nothing."

"All right." Roy smiled. "Food will be here soon. Want something to drink?"

"Sure."

"Beer? Wine? Water? Juice?"

"I think just water, thanks."

"No problem. Come on out. We can eat in the kitchen."

I followed him. He had removed his smock and washed his hands. He wore a gray V-neck T-shirt and looked absolutely scrumptious. His muscular forearms were a work of art.

"Have you ever painted yourself?" I asked.

"A self-portrait? No."

"You should."

"Why?"

"Because you're so..."

He grinned. "So...what?"

"You know exactly how good-looking you are, Roy. You don't need me to tell you."

"What if I *want* you to tell me?" he teased.

Embarrassment welled in me. I could actually feel the

warmth creeping up my cheeks. I hoped it was disguised by the redness from my recent shower.

"I've told you how beautiful *you* are, Charlie."

He had, at that.

"You told me you're an artist," he continued.

"An *amateur* artist."

"Amateur? What does that mean? Either you're an artist or you're not."

"You know exactly what it means. I don't make any money as an artist, and I don't paint full-time."

"Semantics. Do you think I paint for money?"

I said nothing.

He continued. "For that matter, do you think anyone buys my work for any reason other than I'm a Wolfe?"

"That's ridiculous. Your work has value beyond your name."

"Yes. It does. To me. To you. Maybe to others. But I don't do it for the money."

"Well, you don't need to. You already have a ton of money."

He laughed then. "You're being purposely obstinate. You know exactly what I mean."

I got indignant then. "I don't buy it, Roy. You can't be an artist just because you say you are."

"Why not?"

I opened my mouth but then realized I had no answer.

He laughed again. "You are absolutely adorable."

"You tell me, then," I said, not willing to let this drop. "What makes an artist?"

"Depends on your definition of artist."

Now he was being ridiculously abstract. "What's yours?"

"I find art in almost everything. Even my brother Reid, who has taken the running of our business to an art form. Even my father, who, though he was an asshole of the highest magnitude, couldn't have made billions without knowing the art of negotiation and dealing."

"Everything's an art to you?"

"In a manner of speaking."

"What exactly is *my* art, then? Dressing up in uncomfortable clothing and doing someone else's bidding?"

"You're obviously good at what you do, or Lacey wouldn't have brought you with her."

"What I do is hardly art."

"I say it is," he laughed. "But we've gotten badly off the subject. Which I think was your intention. You're certainly willing to go to a lot of trouble just to get out of telling me what you see when you look at me."

I joined in his laughter then. "Nothing gets by you."

"Nothing does," he agreed. "Sometimes that's a curse. Trust me."

His words were enigmatic, and I wasn't sure what to say. I was certain he didn't want to elaborate, so finally I said, "You're the most amazing-looking man I've ever seen."

I 'd made her uncomfortable, which pleased me. Why? I wasn't sure. I hadn't meant to mention that my gift of observation could sometimes be a curse.

I couldn't be an artist without such an acute sense, but truly, it had been a curse from time to time. One time in particular, which I didn't want to think about now. Not when I had a luscious woman in my apartment. I opened my mouth to ask her to elaborate on what she found amazing about my looks, when my intercom buzzed.

"That'll be our food," I said, walking to the door.

I quickly paid and brought the food to the kitchen, where Charlie had taken a seat at my small table. I pushed the newspaper and several books to the side.

"Sorry for the mess."

"No worries. Looks like my place." Then she reddened. "I didn't mean... My place is nothing like this. It's tiny, and—"

"Charlie, it's okay. I know what you meant." I pulled containers of food out from the bag.

"Is there anything I can do?" she asked.

"Nope." I stood and brought some paper plates and plastic utensils to the table. "Not too classy, huh?"

"Classy enough. No dishes to do. Of course, not a friend to the environment."

"These are all recyclable."

"Oh. Good."

I handed her a plate of food. "I hope you like it."

She inhaled. "It smells divine, and as you can tell from my stomach's behavior earlier, I'm famished."

I smiled. Listening to her tummy growl while I was painting her had given her a human side that actually helped me. I'd been thinking of her as this ethereal creature, something above humanity, because of her dazzling silver eyes.

As I looked at her now, I couldn't process how she didn't see her own beauty, which was why I'd wanted her to describe mine.

If she could see mine and put it into words, maybe she could begin to see her own. She'd called me amazing-looking, and while it was a huge compliment and warmed me—a lot—she hadn't actually done what I'd asked.

"Go ahead and eat," I said. "Later you can tell me what it is about me that pleases your senses."

She stared at me then. Stared hard. "There's nothing about you that doesn't please my senses—if you're talking about the five senses, I mean."

"Why are you limiting it to the five senses?"

She reddened. "Well, you were kind of rude when I got here."

"It was nine at night."

"I know."

"Maybe you were rude for showing up at a virtual stranger's house at that hour."

I berated myself inwardly. Why was I reverting to asshole

mode? I was attracted to this woman. I liked her. I'd just fucked her, for God's sake.

She huffed. "It's New York!"

"So?"

She put down her plastic fork and shook her head. "You know, I'm starving, but I'm not going to sit here and take this shit from you. I can't believe I let you fuck me. This is not who I am."

I had to fix this. Quickly. God, I sucked with women.

I searched frantically inside my brain for the perfect words to say, but all I could come up with was, "Don't go."

"Why shouldn't I?

Yeah, I needed an answer to that. An answer that wouldn't paint me as an asshole with zilch experience with women.

"Because you're hungry." I said.

"You're unbelievable." She stood. "I'm starving. You're right. But suddenly the company is making me kind of nauseated."

"Don't go," I said again, this time more strongly. "Please."

"Please? Why? You tell me I'm beautiful. You make love to me. You order me food at midnight. You speak in beautiful words about art and about life...but then you can't stop yourself from being a jerk. What's up with you, anyway?"

If only I could give her an honest answer.

But I couldn't. Not now. Not ever.

"I want you to stay. I want you to eat until you're full and satisfied. And then I want to take you into my bedroom."

"I have work tomorrow."

"So do I."

"You don't work there."

"Still, I work. Besides, there's another big meeting tomorrow at ten, during which I suspect we'll get just as much nothing done as we did today."

That made her laugh—an adorable laugh because clearly she hadn't wanted to laugh at all.

I smiled at her.

"You're impossible," she said.

"I won't deny it."

"I'm going to finish my dinner. Then I'm leaving."

"Have it your way, but you're not going anywhere until you tell me what you find so amazing about me."

She regarded me, an indignant look on her face, and then she shoveled pad thai into her mouth. She was challenging me. Challenging me to make her say something. Challenging me to make her stay.

Fine. I'd accept the challenge. We sat quietly as we both finished our food.

When both our plates were clean, I met her gaze.

She swallowed, placed her plastic utensils on top of her empty paper plate, and returned my stare.

"Your eyes," she said. "They're so dark they're almost black, and I swear to God they get darker when you look at me as intensely as you are now. I know that's physically not possible, but they do. Your hair. So long and silky. It's perfect. Not one tiny bit of frizz. Women would kill to have that hair, Roy. Your nose is perfectly aquiline, reminiscent of Michelangelo's *David*. And those forearms... Muscular and corded. You know? Other women can have their biceps and traps. Give me a good forearm any day."

I nearly opened my mouth to ask what was wrong with my biceps and traps, but then remembered she hadn't seen them. I'd been fully clothed when we'd fucked in the studio, and I'd changed my shirt while she was in the shower.

"Today, when I met you and you were wearing a suit with no tie... I love that look on a man. You could have been walking the runway somewhere alongside your sister. I can't believe no one ever tried to get you into modeling."

Indeed, Riley's agent had tried to get me into modeling, but few knew that.

"And," she continued, "as good as you looked then, when I saw you tonight, your hair up in that stupid man bun—"

I opened my mouth, but she shushed me.

"Yeah, stupid man bun. I always thought they were stupid, until I saw you with one. With your hair up like that, paint smudging your chin, an art smock over a casual shirt and then faded jeans and bare feet... You were magnificent. That was Roy in his natural habitat. As good as you looked dressed to the nines, you looked a thousand times better in your element. As an artist. That was the real you, Roy, and the real you is magnificent."

I sat, awestruck.

This woman had *seen* me. She'd truly seen me, and I wasn't talking about her description of my physical attributes. I wasn't sure anyone else had ever seen the real me with such clarity. Of course she'd never see the inside of my head—that part of me that held secrets I could never reveal, that part of me that haunted me when I let it surface. I'd kept it buried so long, and I'd gotten pretty good at it.

Until my father's murder.

That had dredged everything up from the deep recesses to the shore again, things I'd learned to ignore, treat as if nonexistent.

Charlie Waters didn't see that part of me. She saw me on the surface and in the shallow end.

That was a good thing. A very good thing. For what she saw wasn't an untruth by any means. I was mostly me when I was painting. Business clothes? Maybe I looked good in them, but they weren't me.

So yes, she saw and interpreted exactly who I was. On the outside and partially on the inside.

The only problem was...

I wanted her to see everything.

I'd finally found someone who moved me in a way I'd never known possible.

And that scared the hell out of me.

CHARLIE

My lower lip trembled. I desperately hoped it wasn't enough for Roy to notice.

What had I done?

I'd gone off and rattled out exactly how magnificent he was. Exactly how amazing he looked, but I hadn't even scratched the surface. I'd touched only on his physical attributes. Roy on the inside was a puzzle. He could say the most beautiful words to me, and then, nearly in the same breath, he could say something completely off-putting.

"Thank you," he said softly. "Thank you for seeing me."

"Anyone who looks at you sees you," I said.

"You know what I mean."

I nodded.

I knew.

"I'd like you to stay the night," he said. "I mean, I'd really like you to, but I understand if you need to leave. I understand you have work tomorrow, and you want to make a good impression your first week."

"I want to make a good impression always," I said. "I find value in the work I do."

He smiled then, and I nearly lost my breath at his beauty.

"And you don't consider it art?"

"Not in the same way your painting is."

His smile faded slightly. "Tell me about *your* art, then."

"I haven't painted in a while."

"Have you lost interest?"

"No. Just time. Seems there's always something more important to get done."

"Are you passionate about these other things you're doing?"

Was I? I enjoyed my work. I liked Lacey, and she treated me well.

"It's not art in the way you mean," I said. "I enjoy it, but no. My work is not my passion. I don't think any little girl dreams about being an executive assistant when she grows up."

He smiled again. "There is art in any job well done."

"I can see that."

"What is your *passion*, silver?"

My insides melted. I'd only met this man today, but when he called me "silver," something imploded inside me. Something real, and something I'd ignored for too long. Rather, not ignored, but tried to settle for not feeling, if that made any sense.

"You going to answer me?"

"Sorry. What was the question?"

"Your passion?"

You. The word was on my tongue, and I had to stop it from tumbling out. Roy Wolfe could hardly be my passion. He and I had only just met.

Still, I longed to say it.

Instead, "I paint. Watercolors mostly."

"A beautiful medium. Not one I ever took to."

"I like the transparency of it."

"Do you have any work?"

"A few. There's one in my apartment. Most of them I've given away as gifts."

"Why give them away? Why not sell them?"

"Are you insinuating that I have to get money for something for it to have worth?" I was deliberately pushing his buttons, and I knew it. I couldn't help smiling.

"Of course not. But if you can make money from your passion, you don't *have* to work."

"Most artists never achieve the fame you have."

"I'm hardly famous."

"People pay for your work, don't they?"

"They do. Some more than others."

"So maybe you're not famous, but you make a living."

Did he? I had no idea. He could be living off a trust fund, for all I knew. None of my business anyway.

"No," he said.

"No? No what?"

"I know what you're thinking. It's what everyone thinks. The answer is no. I don't live off Wolfe money. My painting pays my bills. Though Wolfe money did buy this place. But I don't live off it day to day."

"That's nice."

"Nice?"

"I mean, nice that you don't need to depend on your painting."

"But I do. I just told you. My father hated that I wasn't interested in the business. He tried to lure me into it at every turn. He bought me this apartment after I refused to live in the Wolfe building, and then he nearly had a stroke when he saw what I'd done to the master suite."

"Why didn't you tell him to shove the apartment up his ass?"

He laughed then. I was growing pretty darned fond of his laugh.

"You may think my man bun is stupid, silver, but I assure you *I* am not. Would you turn it down if your parents bought you a place?"

"It's a moot point. My mother can't afford to buy me a place." My father could, but that was another story.

"It's hypothetical. What if she could? Would you turn it down?"

"It's a tough question."

"Why?"

"Because I pride myself on my accomplishments. No one has ever given me anything, Roy. I didn't go to college because I didn't want to take loans. Instead, I took paralegal courses at a community college, and the job with Lacey is my first."

"You're evading the question," he said. "Don't try to make me feel less worthy because I allowed my father to pay for my home."

"Why are we fighting about this? Is it really that important?"

"It is to me."

"Why?"

"Because you're making me feel..." He shook his head with a sigh. "Never mind. It doesn't matter."

Then I knew.

He was feeling inadequate. Inadequate because he'd taken money from his father. Money that now belonged to him—as long as Rock stayed at his position as CEO of the company.

Did that bother Roy? That Derek had chosen Rock instead of him? They were both wayward sons. Roy hadn't left town, but he was no more involved at Wolfe Enterprises than Rock had been.

Maybe that was why...

I shook my head. I was making things up now.

"All right, Roy. If my mother bought me a home, I'd probably take it. I'm not an idiot. It's just that the concept is so foreign to me. It's unreal."

"I'm sorry," he said.

"Why? I never wished for a different life."

"No. I mean I'm sorry I pushed it. It's not important. I let my father buy this place. He was trying to bribe me into giving up art. I knew I'd never do that, so I kind of took this place under false pretenses. That made me feel a little better about it."

Such an interesting person.

I'd uncovered a lot about him in the short time we'd been acquainted.

But there was so much more there. So much more I wanted to know.

Would he let me in?

"I want you in my bed," I said.

She smiled. "I know. You've told me. But—"

I quieted her with a gesture. "Not tonight. I know you have to be in early tomorrow, and it's already nearly one a.m. Tomorrow. Come here for dinner. I'll have a surprise for you."

"Roy..."

"You don't have to sleep with me," I said. "That's not what this is about."

"But you just said—"

"I know what I said. It's the damned truth. I want you in my bed more than I've ever wanted another woman. It's crazy, but it's true. But I want something else too."

Something I'd never be able to make happen. I wanted to share my whole self with her, but that would never happen. Even if it could, it was still too soon. I didn't know her well enough to trust her.

Yet.

I wanted to trust this woman. I wanted to trust her with everything.

Maybe someday...

But probably not. Still, I could come close. Closer than I had with anyone else.

I could give *her* something, as well. Something she wanted, something she needed, something she coveted and didn't even realize it.

"Tomorrow," I said.

"But what about...tonight? I mean, it's late, and—"

"I'll take you home, silver. I'd never let you leave here alone this late. It's a good neighborhood, but this is still New York."

"I can call a cab."

"Nope. I'll take you. Plus, I have an ulterior motive."

"What's that?"

"This way I can find out where you live."

"Ha! You can find out anyway the same way I did. Check the employee files."

I smiled. "You forget. I don't work there. This way is much easier."

"So you're giving me the boot?"

"Only for now."

"What about—"

"I want to wait. Until tomorrow. You'll see why when you come back."

"Uh...okay. I guess I'll get my clothes back on, then. Though I hate to give up this glorious robe."

"Keep it," I said. "I have more."

She smiled, rubbing the plush collar against her cheek. "No, I'll leave it here. I kind of like having something here."

I kind of liked it too.

"Your call," was all I said.

She walked toward the bedroom.

I was tempted to follow her. My cock was hard as a rock beneath my jeans, and I could easily fuck her into oblivion, but

I'd meant what I said. I had something special in mind for tomorrow. Something we'd both enjoy.

A few minutes later, she came back out fully clothed in her stiff office garb, her hair pulled back into a high ponytail once more. A shame. She looked the most beautiful with it down, in disarray around her creamy shoulders.

"My car is downstairs in the parking garage."

"Okay. Lead the way."

HER APARTMENT WAS in a converted brownstone.

"It's a studio. All I can afford," she said, reaching for the door handle. "Thanks for the ride. And...for everything."

"I'll see you up," I said.

"You can't stop here. You'll get a ticket."

"It's the middle of the night."

"You still might get a ticket."

"So? Then I'll pay the ticket. It won't be the first parking ticket I've gotten, and I'm sure it won't be the last."

She smiled. "Okay. It's sweet of you to...see me up."

I hurried out of the car and made it to her door just as she was opening it.

"Wow. A gentleman."

"My father may have been a first-class shithead, but he did teach my brothers and me how to treat women." I frowned, remembering. "Actually, that was my mother, not my father."

"Oh?"

"Yeah." We walked up to the concrete steps leading into the brownstone, and Charlie quickly put in a code. I opened the door for her. "Connie Wolfe was nothing if not the etiquette queen. She had an image to uphold. To the public, at least, and her sons were going to be perfect little gentlemen."

"Even Rock?" she asked.

"Even Rock. Until he left."

"Why did he leave, Roy?"

"You'd have to ask him," I said. "None of us know, and he's not exactly forthcoming."

"Your parents didn't tell you?"

"They told us he'd gotten into some trouble and they sent him off to military school. But that's not the whole story."

"How do you know?"

"Because he wouldn't be the first pampered rich boy to get into trouble. Usually the mom and dad buy off whoever they need to, and the kid ends up in a different boarding school to wreak havoc in a new place."

"Oh." She stopped walking. "This is my door. I didn't mean to pry."

"It's okay. But if it's the same to you, I'd rather not talk about my brother."

"What do you want to do, then?"

I cupped her silky cheek, gazing into those sparkling silver eyes. "This."

11

CHARLIE

His lips came down onto mine in a soft kiss. A gentle kiss. Not the raw kiss of untamed passion we'd shared earlier.

This was sweet. Gentle. A promise of something to come.

Something I was definitely looking forward to.

Still, this man was a riddle in human form. Did he truly think *anything* could be art? He seemed to talk in circles. I wasn't sure what he actually believed.

But this was new, for both of us. I had all the time in the world to discover what made Roy Wolfe tick.

Too soon, he ended the gentle kiss, our tongues parting.

I pulled out my key and unlocked the door. "You want to..."

He shook his head. "Until tomorrow, silver." He gave a mock salute and walked toward the staircase.

I watched him until he was out of sight.

MY PHONE ALARM rang too damned early the next morning. I managed to make it into the office by eight, though, and already Lacey had piled the work on for me.

"We're meeting in the same conference room at ten," she said. "I need this stuff before then."

"I'll get right on it." I sighed and began to tackle the comprehensive list.

A few minutes later, she appeared in my doorway. "What did you decide?"

"About what?"

She entered and closed my door. "About Roy."

"Oh." I'd nearly forgotten that I'd asked her about him yesterday. "I guess I'll go for it if he's still interested."

I felt bad lying to her, but Roy was such a recluse, and part of me felt like this was still too new. I didn't want to share it. I wanted it to be mine and only mine for a little while. To tell anyone about it would taint it.

I was being silly, but still...

"I don't know Roy very well," Lacey said, "but I do know that he wouldn't have approached you if he weren't truly interested. He's kind of shy."

"Well, he's an artist," I said, as if that explained everything. In truth, it explained nothing.

"True."

Good. She'd bought it.

"Sorry to pile so much on you," she said. "It's only your second day and all."

"No worries. I'll get it done as quickly as I can."

She nodded and then left my office, leaving the door open. Wolfe Enterprises seemed to have an open-door policy, which was fine with me. I wasn't used to having my own office anyway.

Two hours passed like two seconds. I'd made a considerable dent in Lacey's list but still had plenty to do. I hoped the meeting in the conference room wouldn't take all day. If I had to stay late and finish Lacey's list, I'd miss dinner with Roy.

I grabbed my laptop for notes and headed to the conference room.

I jerked. Only Roy sat inside the room, in the same chair he'd used yesterday. He was dressed to the nines once more, this time in a navy-blue suit and black button-down. No tie. His hair was combed into a smooth low ponytail.

I cleared my throat. "Hi."

He smiled. "Hi, silver."

"You can't—"

"Call you that when everyone gets here. I know." He looked at his watch. "Right on time. Where is everyone else?"

"I don't know. I didn't check Lacey's office before I came."

"I'm sure they'll be here soo—"

Reid walked in the door then. "Hey. Where's Rock?"

"Isn't your office right next to his?" Roy asked.

"He wasn't in it. I assumed he was here."

Jarrod and Terrence arrived behind Reid and sat with me on the other side of the table.

"Hi, Charlie," Jarrod said. "Hanging in there?"

I smiled. "Trying."

I looked over at Roy and his gaze was stern. Had Jarrod been flirting with me? He was just a flirtatious kind of guy, from what I'd seen so far. He was also gorgeous. And single.

I smiled inside. Roy was jealous.

I liked that. I liked it a lot.

Roy didn't have anything to worry about. Jarrod and Terrence were both handsome, but Roy was something else altogether.

"Where the hell is our brother?" Reid said to Roy.

"How the hell should I know? Don't you have him on a leash?"

Reid rolled his eyes. "I wish."

A few more minutes passed in awkward silence, and then Rock and Lacey entered, looking flustered. Lacey's hair was in disarray, and one part of Rock's shirttail was hanging outside his trousers.

"For God's sake," Reid said.

I held back a giggle. Things had apparently not changed since that first time with Rock and Lacey in her former office.

Lacey took her seat, her cheeks red. She still didn't know that I'd heard her and Rock that first day, during a break in the reading of Derek Wolfe's will.

"This is an office," Reid said.

Rock didn't reply, just took his seat at the head of the table. "I've got some people joining us today," he said.

"Who?" Reid asked. "We've got enough to do as it is."

"Some friends of mine from back home."

"This is your home now, Rock," Reid said. "Unfortunately for all of us."

"You're telling me." Rock riffled his fingers through his short hair. "But this is important. They have information for us."

"Who are they?" This time from Roy.

"One's a lawyer, the other's a gynecologist. I've finally convinced them to tell me what they know. At least I think I have."

"Why would anyone in Montana know—"

Rock interrupted Reid. "One of Manny's patients—"

"Wait a minute." This time Reid interrupted Rock. "Manny? Seriously?"

"Yeah, Manny. Hoss and Manny. Make fun of their names now, before they get here."

"And you couldn't have briefed us on this, say...yesterday?" Reid asked. "Maybe during that silent hour you called lunch?"

"Fuck off, Reid," Rock said.

"Rock," Lacey admonished.

"Sorry." Rock cleared his throat. "Manny has a patient who somehow knew I had left Montana. I didn't tell anyone. At first, he wouldn't tell me who it is. Doctor-patient privilege and all. But I think I've convinced him."

"With money?" Roy asked.

"Is there any other way?"

"What does this have to do with anything?" Reid said.

"Don't you get it? She knew I had left Montana for New York. I didn't tell anyone, Reid. Not a fucking one."

"How did your old girlfriend know then?" Reid asked.

Good question. Lacey had told me about Rock's ex, Nieves Romero, who'd shown up a few days after Rock had.

"We're thinking from this person," Lacey said.

"Maybe the patient is Nieves herself," Roy said.

Rock chuckled, shaking his head. "Nieves wouldn't go near Manny naked. When you meet him, you'll see—"

A knock on the conference room door interrupted him. "Come in," Rock said.

Carla, Rock's secretary entered, followed by two men, one tall and thin and the other short and stout.

"Hey, guys," Rock said. "Take a seat. Thanks, Carla."

She nodded and left, closing the door behind her.

"Everyone, meet Horace Stiers and Parker Manfred, better known as Hoss and Manny."

Roy chuckled under his breath and was met with a glare from Reid.

I held back my own chuckle. Hoss and Manny? Really?

Rock introduced the rest of us to the newcomers and bade them to have a seat.

"I hear you have information for us," Reid said.

"Hoss is here as my attorney," Manny said. "I've decided to

tell you what you need to know, but we need to be sure of full confidentiality."

"We can't offer full confidentiality," Rock said. "You know that. We need to talk to this woman."

"She can't know you got her name from Manny is all," Hoss said. "And we can give you the name, but she won't talk to you over the phone. Only in person."

"We'll fly her out," Rock said. "No problem."

"Well...there *is* a problem," Hoss said.

This man looked like he was going to spit a wad of chew any second.

"What's that?" Rock asked.

"She won't travel. You'll have to go to Montana."

"And you couldn't have told us this over the phone?" Reid asked.

"And miss out on a trip to New York, all expenses paid?" Hoss chuckled.

Yeah, this room was going to be a spittoon at any moment.

"Fucker," Rock said, laughing.

"You think this is funny?" Reid asked, his face turning red.

Roy spoke up then. "I think it's a little funny."

I bit my lip to keep from laughing. Even Lacey had covered her mouth, her shoulders quivering.

"You do this shit just to torture me, don't you, Rock?" Reid said, still red in the face.

"I had nothing to do with this. This is all Hoss and Manny."

"So you just gave out a free trip to Manhattan to a couple of clowns."

"Clowns who have information we need. Hell, I flew them coach, and we damned well could afford first class."

"We were expecting the private jet," Hoss said.

"For you bozos?" Rock said. "I don't think so."

Hoss was as tall and skinny as Manny was round. They

laughed uproariously, seeming to focus on Reid, who looked really pissed off.

Rock turned to his friends then. "Let's get serious now. I've already paid you two a shit ton of green. What's up with this?"

Hoss smirked. "Just wanted to see New York."

"Well, see as much as you can today, because you're going back tomorrow. Lace and I will come with you."

"I can't, Rock. I have appointments all day tomorrow. Appointments *you* set up for me."

"Shit. You're right." He looked to Reid.

"Don't even think it," Reid said. "I have better things to do."

Then to Roy, "I guess it's you and me, bro. Want to see Montana again?"

A cannonball hit my stomach. Lacey had told me Roy had slept with a woman in Montana a few weeks ago. Not that he was going to go and rekindle a one-nighter, but—

"I have stuff planned," Roy said.

"For God's sake. Jarrod can't come along. I've got tons of paperwork for him."

Jarrod smiled. "Hey, I'm happy to go."

"Nice try," Rock said. "Lacey, can you spare Charlie?"

"I suppose so, if it's that important you have someone along."

Roy regarded me tersely. He wanted me to turn Rock down. He seriously wanted me to turn down a request from the CEO on my second day on the job.

Not going to happen.

"Okay, Charlie," Rock said. "You and I leave tomorrow. Company jet."

Roy looked down at his computer. He wasn't happy. Surely I'd hear all about this tonight when I met him at his place for dinner.

∾

I MANAGED to escape the office by seven p.m., and I quickly changed into a sundress and sandals in the ladies' room before I headed to Roy's place. I grabbed a cab quickly and made it by seven-thirty.

Roy buzzed me up without so much as a word.

Why was he pissed at me? I couldn't help what Rock wanted. And I did seem to be the only person available on such short notice.

I knocked softly, remembering how I'd come over on a whim just last night, feeling terrible because I hadn't accepted Roy's dinner invitation.

Now, less than twenty-four hours later, I'd had a portrait painted by Roy Wolfe. Oh, and I'd fucked him.

Surreal.

He held the door open for me, still saying nothing. Was that how this evening was going to go? The silent treatment?

I inhaled. Italian. "Smells great. Did you cook?"

"Yeah."

"Lasagna?"

"Baked ziti."

"Sounds great."

"Mmm-hmm."

"What's this about, Roy?"

"What's *what* about?"

"You know damned well what I'm talking about. We had a great time last night—at least I did—and now you won't speak to me."

"You're right. I'm sorry. You want some wine? Chianti?"

"I'd love a glass of wine." Anything to take the edge off. "You have some too."

"I'm not much for wine. Bourbon for me."

"With baked ziti?"

"With just about everything. All three of us are bourbon

drinkers. Reid and I always have been, and Rock is as well. We found that out when he came back here for the reading of our dad's will." Roy chuckled. "He drank a lot of bourbon that night."

"Can you blame him? His whole life was upended."

"No, I can't blame him. I feel for him, actually. I'm damned glad my father didn't decide to foist his company on me. I'd suck at being a CEO."

"Does Rock suck?"

"Strangely, no. He seems to be handling it pretty well. Reid's still pissed, though. He has to bring Rock up to speed on everything for a job he feels should be his."

"I know." Lacey had told me the whole story. It was crazy, but to keep the inheritance in the family, Rock had to relocate here and head up the enterprise.

"I don't know my older brother very well," Roy said. "He seems happily married, though. Crazy about Lacey."

"Then why are you worried about me going off with him?"

"Who says I am?"

"Are you kidding?" I held back a giggle. "It was written all over your face in the conference room. And when I got here, you would barely speak to me."

"I just... I had this whole thing planned for tonight."

"We still have tonight. I don't leave until tomorrow."

"I know. Still..."

"You've gone to the trouble to make dinner and it smells delicious. Let's not spoil it."

"Okay." He handed me my wine and then picked up his glass of bourbon. "To a night you'll never forget, silver."

I smiled and clinked my glass to his. "To a night neither one of us will forget."

His meal was simple yet delicious. A mixed green salad with balsamic vinaigrette, the ziti, and garlic parmesan toast. I ate minimally, as I didn't want that "stuffed" feeling for what was coming. Last thing I needed was a tummy bulge while we were frolicking naked.

"I have some sorbet for a light dessert," he said when he cleared the dishes—paper again.

"Maybe later," I said.

"Sounds good." Then he took my hand and pulled me into a stand next to him. "Ready for something amazing?"

My nerves skittled across my skin as a warmth pulsed through me, landing between my legs. "Absolutely."

He kissed my forehead. "Follow me."

I eyed the door to his bedroom as he led me, my hand in his. I held back a gasp when he stopped in front of the door to his studio instead.

Well, whatever worked for him would work for me. After all, we'd fucked in there last night. Perhaps he'd take me up against the wall again. That was hot. Or maybe we'd go into the master suite bathroom and fuck in the bathtub. Or maybe—

He opened the door. "Surprise, silver."

12

ROY

Her mouth dropped open.

I'd set up an easel with some cotton watercolor paper and a fresh set of colors. I brushed my lips over hers and whispered. "I want you to paint. I want you to paint me."

"But I—"

I touched my fingers to her lips. "Be an artist, Charlie. Be who you were meant to be." I unbuttoned my shirt.

"What are you doing?"

"I'm going to pose for you."

"Naked?"

"I was thinking shirtless." I pulled my hair out of the low ponytail and let it drape over my bare shoulders. "But I'm up for anything."

Her cheeks turned an adorable shade of pink. "I haven't done this in ages."

"An artist remembers. Your hands will remember."

"But I painted buildings. Landscapes. Flowers. Never a portrait."

"Same rules. Paint what you see. Or what you don't see."

"Abstract? I was never much into abstract." She looked down at the palette of color. "Roy, I—"

"This is for you," I said. "If you don't want to do it, you don't have to." Though I was secretly crushed. I honestly thought she'd enjoy this.

"No, it's not that." She shook her head. "This is... This is the nicest thing anyone has ever done for me. Truly."

My heart warmed.

"I just don't know if I... I can't possibly compare to you, Roy."

"Why would anyone, especially me, want to compare you to me?"

"Well, you'll see what I'm doing."

"Not if you don't want me to."

"Really? You wouldn't look?"

"Honey, do you have any idea how long it took me to be able to show someone else my work?"

"How long?"

"Other than family, no one saw my work until I got to college."

"Still, you were younger then than I am now."

"True. But I'd been painting since I could walk."

She smiled, her cheeks still blushed.

"Your work is yours. If you don't want to share it, then don't."

"You're..."

"What?"

"You're...amazing. That's all. I'm just afraid..."

"Of what?"

"That you'll see I'm a talentless hack next to you."

"No two artists are the same."

"Yeah, but some have talent, and others don't."

"If you enjoy art, you probably have talent. You wouldn't do it otherwise. But that doesn't even matter. I told you I won't look if you don't want me to."

"You wouldn't even be the slightest bit curious?"

I laughed. "I didn't say that."

The edge of jealousy was still there. I didn't want Charlie flying off with my big brother tomorrow. But something dawned on me. How easily I laughed when I was in her company.

I'd laughed more in the last couple days than I had in years.

It felt good. Damned good.

"So you *do* want to see it."

"Of course I want to see it! I'm an artist. I love art. I love looking at art."

"Makes sense."

"But I won't look if you don't want me to. Please, Charlie. Paint. Be an artist. Be true to yourself."

She smiled again.

Then she began mixing colors.

"OKAY." She set down her palette. "Done. For now. Some of it needs to dry before I continue."

I nodded. "All right."

Watercolor wasn't a medium I used a lot because of that very thing. I tended to like immediate results. I didn't have the patience to let something dry before I moved on.

She rubbed at a few marks on her forearms. "Nice thing about watercolor. It's a lot easier to clean up than oils."

"True."

I walked toward her, consciously avoiding looking at her work, though I had to force myself.

Honestly? I didn't care if the portrait sucked. I cared that she painted it.

But I'd promised I wouldn't look, so I didn't.

I pulled her away from the easel and pressed my lips to hers.

"How did it feel? How did it feel to have a brush in your hand again?"

She closed her eyes. "It was...heavenly."

"It's a part of you, isn't it?"

"Yeah. It works through me."

"Charlie. Silver. Those are the words of an artist." I kissed her again. "Come with me."

I led her through my bedroom to the small bathroom and turned on the shower. "Just rinse off."

Her eyes widened. "Aren't you going to join me?"

I smiled. "If you insist."

We undressed quickly and walked under the warm pelting water. I eased her hair out of her ponytail and then ran my fingers through it as it got wet.

My cock had jutted out in a full erection. Naked Charlie did that for me. Actually, it had been straining against my jeans during the entire sitting.

She reached forward and touched my hair, now flattened against my head and shoulders by the water. "You have the most beautiful hair, Roy."

I smiled. "You've told me."

"I'll say it again and again. You're magnificent."

The Wolfes were genetically gifted. It was common knowledge. Derek and Connie Wolfe made pretty kids. None of us could deny it.

But to hear Charlie Waters say I was magnificent took it to a whole new level.

I wasn't magnificent. Maybe my looks were. Riley's sure were, and I was supposedly the male version of her.

But magnificent wasn't just on the outside. To be truly magnificent, the inside had to be a part of it. And on the inside, I was broken. Tormented by a secret I still hadn't let out.

Derek Wolfe was dead. He couldn't harm me.

But the others?

I didn't know who or where they were, whether they still existed.

If I spilled what I knew—those facts I kept buried in the innermost part of me, so buried that I didn't even allow myself to think them—bad things could happen.

If something happened to me, I could handle it. At least I liked to think I could. But my brothers and sister?

I couldn't be responsible for anything befalling them. Riley was dealing with her own pain. She had issues I still didn't fully understand. Rock, although newly married and seemingly happy, was also hiding something. I was sure of it. And Reid? He was a loaded gun. He'd had his birthright stripped from him and was prone to being an asshole anyway. Of the four of us, Reid was most like our father.

Which was a scary prospect.

"Roy?" Charlie cupped my cheek.

I jerked out of my thoughts.

"You okay? You were staring into space."

The warm water soothed me, and her touch soothed me even more.

"I was staring at you."

"Nice try. You were a million miles away for a minute."

"I'm here now." I bent my head and captured her mouth.

She opened her soft lips and I swept my tongue around hers. Her tongue was so soft and inviting. So perfect against my own. Her lush breasts crushed against my chest as our bodies slid together under the warm droplets of water.

I kissed her, banishing the troubling thoughts from my mind.

And I knew one thing for sure.

I was going to Montana with her tomorrow.

13

CHARLIE

His kisses were magic. Pure magic. How else to describe something that transported me to another world—a world without anything negative.

Bliss.

Pure bliss.

Our lips slid together as he deepened the kiss. How long had we been standing under the water? The last bit of watercolor on my body swirled down the drain. I clung to Roy, gripped his broad and muscular shoulders, tangled my fingers in his wet hair.

We kissed, and we kissed, and we kissed.

Until the water became lukewarm.

Even then, he didn't pull from the kiss, just eased me out of the shower and turned off the water.

Still he kissed me as he pulled a giant cotton towel from the chrome rack and wrapped it around both our bodies. Though his hands were busy, our mouths never separated.

Finally, I had to pull away and inhale.

The hell with an inhale. That was a gasp.

Water dripped onto my shoulders and chest from my wet hair. Roy smiled and handed me a smaller towel.

I squeezed as much water as I could out of my hair and into the towel as he did the same.

Then I looked at him. Just looked at this incredible man, his damp hair sticking to his shoulders, his cock huge and erect, even his large feet perfectly formed and beautiful, not a callus in sight.

He stroked his index finger down my cheek and over my jawline. "You're absolutely breathtaking, silver."

What did he see in me that was so special?

I thought back to the portrait I'd begun in his studio. Yes, the techniques had come back to me. Yes, I'd been moderately pleased with the result so far. But I'd never be satisfied with it.

I'd never be in the same artistic class as Roy Wolfe.

Never in a million years.

The man was a genius. He had painting in his soul. His work spoke to me—to everyone—on so many different levels.

Then I couldn't help smiling. The gorgeous abstract he'd created just last night, his depiction of me, hadn't satisfied him.

He didn't think he got my eyes right.

How could he not know that he'd glorified my eyes? Made them so much more than they were in reality?

Was an artist never satisfied with his work?

Was I no different from him?

Emotion coiled through me. I was feeling something. Something new. Something vibrant and real and a little bit scary.

It wasn't love. It was way too soon for that.

But this man had awakened something in me. Something I'd never known and could have never even imagined.

"Roy."

"What, silver?"

"Take me to your bed."

He didn't pick me up and hoist me over his shoulder. No. I could imagine Rock doing that, but not Roy.

There was a gentleness about Roy. Not in a sissy way, of course. But in a gentlemanly way. No, that wasn't right either.

He was an artist.

And he'd make love like an artist.

Last night had been fast and furious in his studio, But tonight...

Tonight I'd experience the real Roy Wolfe.

I couldn't wait.

He took my hand, entwining our fingers together, and led me out of the bathroom and into the bedroom. We were already undressed, which disappointed me in a way. How I'd have loved to peel each layer of clothing from him, exposing his majestic body inch by inch.

Or grab both sides of his shirt and rip it off him, making the buttons fly.

Or command him to strip for me and then ogle him as he disrobed, teasing me.

Maybe I'd do all those things in the future.

Maybe.

Would there be more than just tonight?

Would we ever have what Rock and Lacey had?

Because damn, what I was feeling was...

No, I'd already decided. It was too soon for love.

Too soon...

He gently pushed me down on the bed, knelt before me, and spread my legs. "I wanted to taste you so badly last night." He inhaled. "You're ripe, silver. Ripe and wet and pink and glistening. I can't wait to bury my tongue deep inside you."

My nipples tightened and my pussy throbbed.

I was so ready. How long had it been since someone had

gone down on me? A long, long time. Blaine hadn't liked it, though he'd had no problem with me blowing him, of course.

The few times I'd experienced it, I'd loved it. *Loved* it.

And now—

"Oh!"

His tongue slid over my clit.

Shit. This wouldn't take long.

I closed my eyes and leaned downward until my back was flat on the bed. If it wasn't going to last long, I sure as hell was going to savor every minute.

"Damn, silver, you taste like heaven."

He nibbled at my clit this time, and then slid his tongue downward, over my slit and back up again.

I gripped the comforter in my fists, tensing my thighs.

"Relax, honey." He kissed my inner thigh. "Relax and enjoy."

Oh, I was enjoying. I was just tense and eager. Couldn't wait. Couldn't wait—

"Fuck!"

Torpedoes shot through me.

Torpedoes that shook me to my core.

How was I coming after only a few seconds? How?

But the how didn't matter. Nothing mattered. Nothing except the explosion Roy was causing in my body, in my heart.

I tingled, the shivers racing from my pussy outward, through my body, my limbs, my fingers and toes.

One big quake took me over.

I moaned. I yelled. What words, I couldn't say. Only emotion emanated from me. All logic, all thoughts, were gone.

When I finally began to descend, my pussy again became my focus. Fingers were inside. Long thick fingers thrusting in and out, in and out, in and out.

And a voice. A deep masculine voice.

"You're so hot, silver. So hot. Keep coming. Keep coming."

I sank then. Sank deep into Roy's mattress, cloaked in sheer delight and contentment.

I could never move again and be completely happy. Hopelessly and blissfully happy.

Then a body hovered above me. A cock sank into me.

And a wave of completeness shrouded me.

Total completeness.

One with this man—this special and amazing man.

His hardness slid in and out of me, his cock burning a tunnel in my tight pussy. So good. So fucking good.

I curled my legs up and around him, resting my calves on his ass as he pumped, his hips pistoning furiously.

Thrust. Thrust. Thrust.

Every tissue in my body was on alert, highly sensitized. Until... Until... Until—

"God!" I screamed as my second orgasm rolled from my clit into my core and then outward to the tips of my fingers.

"Yes! Oh, God, yes!"

"That's it, silver. God, I can feel your pussy sucking against my cock. Feels so good. So good. So goo—"

He pushed his cock into me balls deep, and my climax continued, pulsing around him.

We came in tandem. Together and joined.

And it was magnificent. Miraculous.

Perfect in every way.

When his cock finally stopped pulsing, he turned and fell onto his back next to me. My legs still hung off the side of the bed.

My body was shiny with perspiration, and my heart thudded rapidly against my chest.

Roy lay immobile, one arm across his forehead, the other resting on my belly.

We stayed there, silent, for a few timeless moments. Until a phone rang.

Roy jerked. "That's me."

He got up and pawed around, looking for his phone, I assumed.

When he finally found it, he said, "Yeah? This is Roy Wolfe."

14

ROY

"It's me. Rock."

"What is it?"

"I need you at the office first thing in the morning. I've set you and Reid up to plan our father's memorial service."

What? This was the first I'd heard of a memorial service. "He's already been cremated, Rock."

"Yeah. I know. But I've been talking to the attorneys, and they feel we need to have a lavish memorial service for our esteemed father. Make it look good, you know?"

"Look good for whom?"

"For everyone, but mostly for the law. Every one of us is implicated, so we need to at least *act* like we care."

"If we cared, we'd have done this before now."

"Maybe. Maybe not. We weren't expecting Dad's death. It was a homicide, so no one will think twice that we didn't have the service the next day."

"They might. This was Derek Wolfe. He could buy anything, including the most expensive memorial service on the planet the day after death."

"Well, that didn't happen. Our story is that we wanted to wait until Riley returned."

"Riley was here when he died."

"Try to keep up with me, Roy. Yes, I know she was here. But now she's not, and that's our plan. We waited a few days for Riley to return, and when she didn't, we went ahead with plans for the service. Got it?"

"Don't treat me like an idiot, Rock. Yeah, I get it. I just don't think anyone in the free world will buy it."

"They'll have to. It's all we've got."

"Why do I have to take part?"

"Because you're a dutiful son."

"Nope. Not doing it. You be the dutiful son."

"Dude, I'm the *only* one who has an ironclad alibi. I wasn't in the state when this all went down."

"So? You're the new CEO of the company. You should take the reins here."

"Then who's going to Montana to meet with our witness?"

"*I* am."

"Why the hell would you want— Oh. I see."

"What?" I asked, trying to sound innocent.

"You have the hots for Lacey's assistant. I thought I saw a look pass between you two today. That's it."

I said nothing.

"No offense, but you don't know these guys."

"Hoss and Manny, you mean?"

"Yeah. And their witness. You won't know what to ask or anything."

"And you will? Or Charlie?"

"Lace is giving me a list of questions."

"Which you can easily give to me."

Silence.

Let him try to discount the logic. He wouldn't be able to.

"Fine. You go."

I smiled into the phone. "When do we leave?"

"Tomorrow morning. Eight a.m. sharp. Be at our private terminal at JFK."

"Got it. We'll be there." I ended the call.

Back to business.

I had a naked woman in my bed.

To my dismay, however, Charlie had fallen asleep.

I smiled and kissed her silky cheek, and then I walked to the studio to have a look—

I stopped just short of the door.

No.

I'd promised her I wouldn't look at the painting.

Normally, I'd think this was an innocent little violation of a promise that didn't mean a whole lot. I mean, seriously. Who cared if I looked at her painting? She'd never know.

Odd.

I knew who cared.

I did.

I fucking cared.

I didn't want to violate Charlie's trust, even over something so minute.

I walked out to the kitchen, ate two spoons full of cold ziti, and drank a glass of water.

Then I joined Charlie in my bed.

THE PHONE ALARM went off at five a.m.

Charlie jerked upward. "What? Where am I?"

"Shh. You're with me, silver. You fell asleep last night, and I didn't want to wake you."

"Oh. Yeah. What time is it?"

"Five o'clock."

"Five? Why did your alarm go off at— Oh, shit! That's right. I have to go to Montana with Rock. I have to get home. Pack. Fuck. Fuck. Fuck."

"Relax. We can buy whatever you need once we get there."

"But I should look professional." She bit her bottom lip. "I still have the suit I wore yesterday in the car. I changed at work before I— Wait. What do you mean *we*?"

"New plan. I'm going with you instead of Rock."

"But you don't work for the company."

"I do today."

"I don't understand."

"Nothing to understand," I said. "I'm helping out."

Did she look disappointed? Did she want me to admit I was going because I didn't want her traveling alone with my brother? Didn't want to have her out of town where I wouldn't see her? I couldn't tell.

Finally, she said, "But I don't have any of my sundries."

"Which you can find at any drugstore."

"But I use a special cleanser. I have really sensitive skin—"

I placed two fingers over her beautiful lips. "We'll find it. We'll find everything you need, and I personally will make sure nothing harms your beautiful skin."

"But—"

"Everything will be fine. Trust me."

"Lacey was supposed to give me the details."

"Check your email. She probably did."

"Of course. What did I do with my purse?" She hopped out of bed, her breasts swaying gently against her chest.

Yeah, I was rock hard.

But we didn't have a lot of time.

Then again, I didn't need a lot of time.

"Come back to bed for a minute," I said.

"No way. We need to get out of here."

"I'm not sure you heard me," I said. "Get the fuck back in bed."

15

CHARLIE

Had I heard him right?

It was the same voice with the same deep timbre.

But his words weren't kind. They were demanding. A little bit of a turn-on, but very unlike Roy Wolfe.

I walked backward until I hit a chest of drawers, the handle of one of the drawers clawing into my back.

"I'm sorry," he said immediately. "I didn't mean that to sound—"

"Okay... But we have to get moving."

"So we don't take off on time. It's a private jet. No big deal."

"But it's my job!"

He didn't get it. Roy had been born with a silver spoon in his mouth. But I wanted to keep this job.

"Your job is safe. Lacey loves you."

"I want her to continue to love me for *me*. Not keep me around because I'm sleeping with the CEO's brother."

"The CEO who happens to be her husband."

This wasn't the Roy I thought I knew. Then I laughed aloud. I *didn't* know him. We'd met exactly forty-eight hours ago. This was crazy.

For a minute, I'd allowed myself to think this could be a fantasy love-at-first-sight story like Rock and Lacey's.

I was wrong.

Rock was who he was. He didn't hide himself from anyone. He came in like a bull in a china closet, made all the waves he could, and didn't apologize for any of it. From what I'd heard in the old office that first day, he was that way in the bedroom as well.

Roy?

Roy was a puzzle.

The soul of an artist and the beauty of a Renaissance sculpture...but something wasn't adding up.

Did I want to know what it was?

Did I?

I exhaled slowly. Last night I'd been fancying myself in love with him. Oh, I hadn't allowed myself to think the words, but that was where I was headed. I'd known it at the time, just hadn't wanted to form the words in my head.

I had to slow down.

Way down.

Of course, getting on a private jet with him and flying to Montana wasn't exactly the way to do that.

But I didn't have a choice.

It was my job.

"Silver..."

"What?"

"You just haven't said anything in a few minutes."

I nodded. Time to get serious. "You might not take this seriously, but I do. This is my job, and I want to do the best I can. I plan to be at the private terminal on time, preferably a little early. What you do is up to you."

"They won't take off without me."

"Doesn't matter. I'll be on time no matter what. I want a good report to go back to Lacey and Rock."

He smiled. "You're something."

"Is that a compliment?"

"Your work ethic. It's wonderful. I actually share it—when it comes to my real work. My art."

"This is just as important as your art right now," I said adamantly. "If we don't solve this case, one of you is going to go down for your father's murder."

"None of us offed the bastard."

"I know that. I believe you. But the cops want someone to pay for this, and if we don't find out who did it—or at least prove you and your siblings didn't—it could happen."

Chills rushed through me at the thought. Roy was big and strong, but he wouldn't fare well in prison. Rock and Reid would do okay, but Roy? There was a vulnerability about him, something I didn't want to see tainted.

Was there, though? Or was I making that up? He seemed to be hiding something. Perhaps I was stereotyping an artist's soul as vulnerable.

Maybe Roy Wolfe was just as strong as his brothers.

Maybe he was stronger.

16

ROY

"I was being selfish," I said. "You look so beautiful, and I'm hard as a rock. I just wanted to have you once more before we left."

"You didn't have to get so demanding about it."

"You don't like to be bossed around in the bedroom?"

She appeared to think for a moment. Then, "Not when I'm running late."

A-ha. When we had more time, I'd try again.

Not that I was any kind of Dominant in the bedroom, but something about Charlie Waters made me want to have all of her on my terms. I wasn't sure why. I'd never had a lot of luck with women, and even when I did get lucky, I performed well but never did I get overly dominant.

My experience was horribly lacking compared to my little brother's. Reid lived up to our last name with a vengeance, and while I knew little of my older brother's antics in the last decade, something told me he'd had his share of bed warmers as well.

I was shy.

Not shy so much as a classic introvert who enjoyed his own company. Especially when I was painting. The colors and brushes became an extension of me—in effect, became me as I created. Art was a solitary endeavor.

I never went looking for anything more than a fuck because I figured I'd always be a solitary. Never have a long-term relationship.

Charlie Waters made me think about a long-term relationship.

And that scared the shit out of me.

I had to keep this casual, for both our sakes.

I had to.

The secret ate me up inside, even though I never let myself see those images that were embedded deep in my mind. Hear those words of so long ago.

My father had deserved his fate, no doubt.

But the others... How many were there? Were they still out there? Did they still have the leverage they once had?

And why was I such a fucking coward?

Didn't matter. Nothing mattered except proving the innocence of my family. We weren't going down for the murder of that bastard. Not on my watch.

Charlie was frantically grabbing her clothes. "I'm going to take a quick shower. Want to join me?"

"If I join you, it won't be quick." I smiled.

"True. Then stay out of the bathroom until I'm done. Give me ten minutes or so. I'll be fresh-faced today. The only makeup I have in my purse is some lipstick and mascara.

"You don't need it. Those silver eyes don't need any other adornment than their natural sparkle."

She giggled and headed into the bathroom.

And I took care of my stubborn hard-on.

～

CHARLIE'S EYES were big as saucers when we boarded the Wolfe Jet. I hadn't used the jet nearly as much as Reid had, but I'd been on board enough times not to be completely entranced by its luxury.

Hell, I'd grown up in luxury. It was nothing new to me. Who needed parental love and devotion when you had luxury like this?

Apparently not the Wolfe kids.

When we reached our cruising altitude, two attendants offered us breakfast, complete with mimosas.

"I couldn't." Charlie shook her head. "It's a work day."

My first instinct was to argue with her, as I had this morning about being on time. But she was right, and I did respect her work ethic.

"No alcohol for me either," I said. "Just coffee."

"Perfect," Charlie agreed.

We noshed on bacon, eggs, and whole wheat English muffins with raspberry jam, hardly conversing at all.

Yet it wasn't awkward, the silence.

It seemed normal.

It seemed...*natural.*

Being with Charlie Waters seemed very natural to me.

"You're cute when you eat." I wiped a tiny smudge of jam from the corner of her mouth.

She swallowed the bite of English muffin. "Cute? Can't say I've ever heard that before."

"You just seem to enjoy food."

"I do. Don't you?"

"Yeah. Always have. We Wolfes have good taste in food. Except Riley. She eats like a bird. She's too thin, I think."

"She's gorgeous," Charlie said. "I'd give my left arm to have her body."

"Haven't you ever noticed how skinny her arms are?"

Charlie cocked her head. "I've never interacted with her, actually. She always looks great to me."

"She's too thin," I said. "Reid and I agree on that. Her agent keeps her on a forced starvation diet. No fat. Pretty much all brown rice and vegetables and the occasional lean piece of fish."

"That's not healthy."

"Damn right it's not." I sighed. "I worry about her."

"Have you tried looking for her?"

I shook my head. "We gave up the last time. When she takes off, she doesn't want to be found."

"You don't think she—"

"Murdered him? No way. She was his little angel. He kicked the shit out of the rest of us."

Charlie jerked in surprise.

"Sorry. You didn't think he was a model citizen, did you?"

"Of course not. I knew none of you were fans, but..."

"You didn't consider *why* none of us were fans?"

"But if Riley was his favorite, and he doted on her, why does she have..."

"Issues? Her diet, probably. Our mother always expected her to be the perfect little mini Connie Wolfe."

"And she was your dad's favorite?"

"God, yes. He whaled on Reid and me. Reid got the worst of it after Rock left. I was a loner. I learned how to avoid him. But Reid got his ass kicked regularly."

"And Riley?"

"He wouldn't dare lay a hand on his perfect princess," I said. "She was everything to him. They went on special trips overseas and everything."

"Wow. Really?"

"Yeah. Reid and I didn't care too much, though. We hated the bastard, and he seemed to hate us. The last thing either of us wanted was to be alone with him anywhere."

"Hmm." She lifted her brow, looking pensive.

"What?"

"If she had such a good relationship with him, why hasn't she been clamoring for a major memorial service sendoff?"

"Well, she's not here, for one."

"Why would she take off now?"

"Who knows? None of us knows why she takes off. Reid and I tried to help her when this first began, but we didn't get anywhere."

"It just seems, if they were so close, as you say, sharing trips and all..."

I shook my head. "Like I told you. I have no idea."

But I did have an idea. An idea I couldn't force to the forefront of my mind for fear of what I'd find there. Those images, those words... The things I couldn't unbury...

But I had to. The time was coming.

If we were all going to find the truth, we needed all the facts.

Even those facts buried deep within my psyche.

The problem was...I wasn't sure what bringing them to the surface would do to me.

And I didn't want to find out.

17

CHARLIE

I was riding in a limo. In a damned limo!

I'd come to Helena in a private jet, and now I was in a Hummer limo, going to the best hotel in the city.

Crazy, this life. So crazy.

Roy sat beside me, dressed in jeans, Italian leather shoes, a white shirt unbuttoned at the top, and a sports jacket.

And my God, he looked scrumptious.

He hadn't come on to me on the plane, a fact which had surprised me quite a bit. We'd talked a lot, mostly about nothing in particular, but some about his family. His brothers and sister.

Riley Wolfe seemed to be as much of a puzzle to her brothers as she was to me.

If she and Derek Wolfe had been so close, why wasn't she here mourning? Or if running off was her way to deal with stress, what had happened the other times she'd run off? How many times had she pulled this? I'd have to ask Roy. If he even knew. He wasn't exactly family-centric.

We pulled into the hotel and the driver opened the door for me and helped me out of the limo. Crazy!

I didn't like the fact that I was wearing the same suit I'd worn yesterday, but no one knew that except Roy, and he didn't seem to care one bit. Why should I?

"Mr. Wolfe, Ms. Waters." A tall and slightly masculine woman greeted us. "I'm Toni Franks, the hotel manager. We're so pleased to have you as guests here. We've got a conference room set up for your meeting in an hour. In the meantime, the bellhops can get you settled in your suite.

Suite? What?

I must have looked surprised, because Roy said, "It's a two-bedroom suite, Charlie."

I jerked for a split second. He almost never called me Charlie. Usually silver, or if not that, honey or baby.

I'd have my own bedroom. In a suite.

A fucking suite!

I tried to contain my exuberance as the bellhop gathered our belongings and we walked into the hotel.

The suite was the ultimate in luxury. I'd thought the private jet was luxurious, but this...

Impeccably decorated with a modern flare, the suite boasted a full kitchen, a living area, a bar, and then closed doors which I assumed led to the bedrooms.

"Right this way, sir, to the master suite," the bellhop said to Roy.

"The master is for the lady," he said.

"Oh, I—"

"No argument, Ms. Waters," he said, his dimples showing. "This is your first trip as a representative of Wolfe Enterprises, and I want it to be a memorable one."

Ms. Waters?

Was that for show?

Roy Wolfe was just as much of a puzzle as his sister was.

The bellhop was tall and blond with a glint in his sparkling blue eyes. "Ms. Waters?" He held out his hand. "Nice to meet you. Have you been to Montana before?"

His handshake was firm. "No, this is my first visit."

"Get out and see it. Get out of the city if you can. There's a reason we call it big sky country. It's gorgeous here."

"I'll try," I said. "I don't know how much time I'll have for pleasure."

"I'd be happy to show you around," he said.

"I'll be showing her around," Roy interjected, handing him a wad of bills. "Thank you."

I couldn't help but smile. Was Roy actually jealous? The bellhop was cute, but he was nothing compared to the majesty that was Roy Wolfe.

I had no idea how long we'd be staying here. I hadn't bothered to ask, and I hadn't brought anything with me other than the sundress I wore last night since I'd gone straight from Roy's place this morning. I assumed it would just be an overnight trip.

Once the bellhop was gone, I turned to Roy. "What now?"

"We have a meeting in less than an hour," he said, a glint in his eye.

"Oh, no. I can't. Not right now. I'm nervous as hell about my first official stint for your company."

"I know a surefire way to combat nerves." He pulled me to him, our gazes locked.

No. I shouldn't. I couldn't. I...wouldn't.

Except I would.

I knew I would.

He crushed his lips to mine.

Our kiss was raw and passionate. We didn't have a lot of time, and we both knew it. We dived into that kiss, our tongues dueling and jousting, our lips sliding together and our teeth clashing.

It was wonderful. A wonderful kiss. And I was getting wet...

He broke the kiss and lifted me into his arms. "God, you drive me insane, silver. Completely insane."

I smiled against his shoulder. I could handle that. I liked it. Loved it, even.

No man had ever said I made him insane.

What insanity did Roy have in mind for me? I couldn't wait to find out.

He pushed through the door to the master suite where the bellhop had taken my bag. "I want to rip those goody-goody clothes off your luscious body."

Yes. Yes, please. But no! "You can't! This is the only suit I have."

"I'll buy you another suit."

"Our meeting is in forty-five minutes!"

He sighed. "Fuck. You'll have to undress yourself, then. I can't be held responsible for what I'll do to those clothes. They aren't you, silver. You belong in that flowing sundress you were wearing last night. Or in simple jeans and a cropped T-shirt. Or short shorts and a tank. Not an uptight suit. Is it even comfortable?"

"Not really. But I've always worked in an office in New York City. This is what I have to wear."

"If you were an artist, you could wear what you want."

I clasped my hand to my mouth. "Did you—"

"No, I didn't look at your painting, though I'll be honest. I was tempted. If it had been anyone but you, I might have."

"Why not me?"

"Because I promised you I wouldn't, silver, and for some reason, I don't want to break a promise to you."

My breath caught.

Of everything he'd said to me in the short time I'd known him, this touched me the most. I wasn't sure why. He'd waxed poetic about my eyes, my breasts, my body, my pussy...but this...

Was this for real?

Was *he* for real?

How could I express in words what feelings he invoked in me without scaring him into running away screaming?

Answer? I couldn't.

So I'd express with my body. I shed each article of clothing quickly and succinctly, placing it all in a neat, though not folded, pile. Then I knelt before him, unbuckled his belt, and unsnapped and unzipped his jeans.

Best thing you could do to show appreciation to a man? Every woman knew the answer.

Give him head.

And that was just what I was about to do.

18

ROY

Her little pink tongue slid out from between her lips and she licked the head of my cock.

And I nearly exploded on the spot.

I hadn't had a lot of women, but every one of them had given me head. Every one of them had exclaimed over the size of my cock.

Charlie Waters hadn't said anything about my cock, but here she was, on her knees, about to take it into her sweet, warm mouth.

I had to keep cool. Had to hold on.

On the other hand, we were in a hurry.

I grabbed the back of her head and gently pushed her toward me, filling her mouth with my dick.

She let me.

She fucking let me.

All my other women had balked at that. Wanted to go at their own pace. Didn't want me leading. I even understood, since it was their mouth and they could easily choke if I wasn't careful.

But Charlie let me push her face toward me, took my cock to the back of her throat.

I wanted to come inside that hot little mouth. But I also wanted to come inside that hot little pussy. In that hot little ass, something I never thought I'd be interested in.

God, but I was. I was interested in everything with her. With this amazing, gorgeous woman who sparkled.

Yeah. That was the word. Charlie Waters sparkled. It wasn't just the silver in her eyes. That was a big part of it, but it went deeper. She was beautiful, from her gorgeous hair to her cute little toes, but she sparkled from the inside out. It was her heart. Her artist's heart. Her good heart.

Emotion coiled through my belly, making me feel slightly nauseated but in a good way. These were powerful feelings—powerful feelings I'd never experienced.

I feared I'd never experience them again.

"Take me." I led her mouth down the shaft of my cock and then off again. "Take all of me."

I wasn't familiar with a lot of cocks, but the few women I'd been with had said I was huge. My little silver was a trouper. She took it all, even held it for a few seconds as I nudged the back of her throat.

I had to give her a break. I let go of her hair to let her set the pace.

And she did. She did exactly as she had been doing. She took me deep, to the back of her throat, held for a few precious seconds, and then released.

God, she drove me crazy. Completely insane. I hadn't been lying when I'd told her that. I was crazy with desire, ready to pump my semen down her hot throat and make her swallow all I had to give.

All of me.

"Yeah. God, honey. Feels so good, the way you suck me."

She moaned at my words, the vibrations humming along my shaft, driving me crazier with passion and need.

Come. I needed to come so bad. Wanted to come so bad. But her pussy. I wanted to eat her pussy. Slap her cute little ass. Fuck her. Fuck her until she couldn't stand.

Then it was happening. The scrunching of my balls, the tightening of my cock, the tiny pulsating nudges, telling me it was time to—

"Fuck! I'm going to come. I'm fucking coming! Take me. Take all of me!"

I exploded in her warm mouth, her tongue twirling along my shaft as I released into her. Would she swallow? Or would she, like the others, hold it in her mouth and excuse herself to spit?

Couldn't worry about that now, not when I was having the most intense orgasm of my life.

It spread through my body like rapid wildfire, teasing me and then taking me flying. Words escaped my throat. What words? I had no idea. Words of praise to the woman doing this to me. Her name. Her beauty. Everything.

When I finally began to come down, she still knelt at my feet, her lips pressing soothing kisses over the head of my cock.

Her sweetness was legendary. Her hotness was out of this world.

This woman.

This beautiful, sparkling woman.

She finally removed her mouth from my cock and met my gaze. I stared into the intense silver, and what I saw there...

I couldn't name it. It was passionate and intense. It was raw and untamed.

It was beautiful.

Utterly beautiful.

Finally, she smiled. "We should get dressed and go."

"But you... I didn't take care of you."

"Later," she said. "We can't be late to this meeting."

"But I'm a Wolfe."

"Well, I'm not." She stood. "And *I'm* not going to be late."

Her work ethic again. An amazing and attractive quality in a woman. I was used to women who were after my money. Women who had no work ethic.

Charlie Waters was not after my money. Of that I could be certain.

She regarded herself in the full-length mirror on the side wall. "Gads! I look awful."

"You could never look awful."

In fact, she looked luscious. I could eat her up. Would be ecstatic to do just that.

She gathered her clothes and headed into the master bath. I was still fully clothed, my jeans and boxer briefs halfway down my thighs. I pulled them up quickly, wincing as they grazed my sensitive cock.

Within five minutes, Charlie emerged from the bathroom looking completely put together. Like she could be on the cover of *Forbes* as a successful businesswoman.

Even though she didn't belong in those uptight clothes, I couldn't take my gaze from her.

She looked like she could conquer the fucking world.

I had no doubt that, one day, she'd do just that.

"You ready?" she asked.

"As ready as I'll ever be."

Lacey had given us questions to ask the woman we'd be interviewing. Though I hadn't relished the idea of Rock making this trip with Charlie, I wished he were here now. Rock might actually know this woman. She had seemed to know him, apparently.

The story was that Manny, a gynecologist, had seen this woman as a patient, and the patient told Manny that Rock had relocated to New York. Since Rock hadn't told anyone he was leaving, this created a puzzle.

Who was this woman? And what did she know?

The images again, blurred as always, tried to fight their way into my brain. What if this woman...?

No, couldn't go there.

But had to.

Had to eventually.

Not today.

19

CHARLIE

Wow. What a conference room! Refreshments, including Champagne, had been set up. My stomach growled, but I took a ladylike portion of fresh strawberries dipped in chocolate and a cup of coffee.

Roy helped himself to a heaping plateful of everything else.

Apparently our guests hadn't arrived yet.

That soon changed with a knock on the door.

The hotel manager from this morning peeked in. "I have a Horace Stiers and Leta Romero to see you."

Roy nodded. "Come on in."

I sat down at my place at the table and turned on my laptop.

Roy stood and held out his hand. "Good to see you again, Hoss. Ma'am, I'm Roy Wolfe."

He sounded so professional. I wasn't sure why I was surprised. Introverts could still be professional.

The woman was lovely—dark hair and eyes with fair skin. She nodded to Roy.

"Please have a seat," Roy said.

They sat awkwardly. Hoss was tall, lanky, and bald. A little creepy looking, actually. Creepier than I remembered.

"Mr. Stiers, you remember our executive assistant, Charlie Waters?"

"Yes, ma'am. Good to see you again."

"And this is Ms. Romero."

I nodded. "Nice to see you both."

"Ms. Romero," Roy continued, "thank you for being willing to speak to us privately like this. I assure you that we will keep this conversation confidential as best we can."

"What do you mean, 'as best you can'?" Hoss asked.

"As you know, my siblings and I have been implicated in our father's murder. If Ms. Romero has information that can exonerate us, we'll need to call her in as a witness."

"I don't even know any of you," Leta said.

"Then how did you know Rock had left Montana?" Roy asked.

"I heard it from my sister."

"Your sister?"

"Yes. Nieves. Nieves Romero."

That piqued my interest. Lacey had mentioned that Rock had a previous girlfriend who'd showed up in Manhattan wanting to start things up again.

"How would she know?"

"She and Rock are close," Leta said.

"In what way?"

"They're sleeping together."

Roy's eyes widened. "My brother's a married man, Ms. Romero."

"What? You think married men don't sleep around?"

"He's newly married, and I don't think he's sleeping around." Roy paused a moment. "We're starting out on the wrong foot. Perhaps your sister and my brother had a relationship in the past, but he's devoted to his new wife now. But it really doesn't matter whether you think your sister is still sleeping with Rock.

We need to know everything."

Her cheeks reddened.

"It's okay," Hoss said.

"Just a rumor," Leta said. "A rumor I heard from my sister."

"Can you elaborate?" Roy asked.

"Well, she's close to Rock, and he said once that…"

"Go ahead," Roy said. "We need to know everything."

"He didn't talk much about his previous life in New York. In fact, he hated talking about it. But once, he mentioned something. About his sister."

"Yes? What about my sister?"

"He said it was because of his sister that he got sent away."

Riley? She'd been all of six when Rock got sent away. What could she have possibly done?

"My sister was six at that time," Roy said, echoing my thoughts.

"She was?" Leta shook her head. "That doesn't make much sense, then."

"No, it doesn't. Perhaps your sister misheard what Rock said. Or perhaps she's lying to you."

"That wouldn't be out of the question," Leta said. "My sister is very self-motivated and isn't above lying to get what she wants."

"How would this lie get her what she wants?"

Leta shook her head. "I have no idea."

"So this is what you said to Manny during your medical examination?" Roy asked.

"Partly, yes."

"What else did you tell him about Rock or the Wolfes?" Roy asked.

"Another rumor I heard from my sister."

"Go on."

"She said there was more to Derek Wolfe than met the eye."

"And did your sister say this came from Rock?"

"Yes...and no."

Roy sighed. "I'm trying to be patient here, Ms. Romero, but you need to give us more detail. Please elaborate."

"She said Rock hated his old man. He wouldn't say much more than that. But Nieves is nothing if not persistent, so she did some research."

"And what did she find?"

"Nothing."

"This is getting us nowhere," Roy said.

"I'm not finished yet," Leta said.

"Go on, then."

Roy held back an eyeroll. I could tell just by looking at him. I continued tapping furiously on my laptop, taking meticulous notes. Also, unbeknownst to Ms. Romero, I was recording her answers. I hadn't planned to, but something inside me made me do it. I could always delete it later.

"Well," Leta said, "Nieves didn't find anything, but then someone called her."

"Who?"

"They didn't give her a name. But they told her Derek Wolfe had been killed."

"They didn't tell her Rock had left Montana?"

"I don't think so. She didn't say that. I think she just inferred that when he didn't answer his phone at the cabin when she tried to call."

"Anything else? A Manhattan billionaire being murdered would be pretty common knowledge, even here in Montana. Why would Nieves already know that?"

"That's the weird thing," Leta said. "The call came an hour before the time of the murder."

20

ROY

"How would she know that?" I asked.

"Not too difficult. Once the murder hit the news and the police figured out when the murder had taken place, Nieves saw that she'd received the call before he'd been killed."

"We're going to need to see her cell phone records," I said to Hoss.

"You'll need a subpoena," he said.

"How about some money, instead?"

"Are you trying to bribe me, sir?" Hoss asked.

"Oh, for God's sake," I said. "This is an unofficial meeting. I'm not a fucking cop. I have no interest in harming Ms. Romero or you. My interest is in exonerating my family, myself included."

"It's okay," Leta said. "I can talk about it. Though maybe you should be talking to Nieves."

"We would be, if we'd known she's the source of your information," I said. "But you're here now. Please go on."

"Nieves didn't think anything of it at the time. It was a voice-mail, so she didn't get it until the next morning, and by then it was on the news. It wasn't until later that she realized the phone call had come before the actual murder. Like I said, after the police had determined the timing."

"Did the voicemail say anything else?"

"Just that Derek Wolfe wasn't who he appeared to be, like I said."

"Did she save that voicemail?"

"I don't know. But if I had to guess, I'd say she did."

"Why do you say that?"

"Because it involved Derek Wolfe, which meant it involved Rock. And if Derek was dead, that meant Rock inherited a lot of cash, and Nieves would want in on that."

"Sounds like you don't think too highly of your sister," I said.

"Actually, we're close, but I know who she is. I doubt she'd deny it."

Charlie cleared her throat, nodding to me.

"Yeah?"

"May I ask Ms. Romero a question?"

"Of course."

"Ms. Romero, are you aware that your sister came to Manhattan the week after Derek Wolfe's murder to see Rock?"

"No, but it doesn't surprise me."

"Has she returned to Montana?"

"I don't honestly know. I haven't seen her, and we use our cells to communicate, so I guess she could be anywhere."

"Why don't you give her a call right now?" I said. "See if she can meet us here."

"I'm not sure I should do that."

"Why not?"

"Because then she'd know I've been blabbing stuff she told me. She wouldn't take kindly to that."

"We're going to call her in anyway," I said. "And if she doesn't cooperate, we'll have the police question her. Would you rather she be arrested?"

"You can't arrest her for getting a voicemail."

She was right. I'd misspoken in my haste. I glanced at the notes from Lacey. I really should stick to them.

"I'm sorry. I meant questioned by the police."

"I was wondering about that anyway," Leta said. "Why am I here? Why didn't you just have the police question me?"

"Because right now, the police consider my siblings and me suspects in the case. None of us had anything to do with it, of course."

"How well do you know your siblings?" she asked.

Bam.

Brick to my gut.

I knew Reid well enough. Riley sort of. Rock? Not really at all. But did I think any of them were killers? Not in a million years.

"Very well," I lied. "My siblings and I had nothing to do with our father's murder. Besides, I believe you're here to answer our questions, and you're being very well compensated."

But there *were* people who would want my father dead...and I wasn't thinking of the myriad associates in the business world he'd pissed off. No, they might want him dead, but they wouldn't kill him.

But people existed who would.

The people in those blurred images I couldn't bring to the front of my mind.

Would the fact that I knew make me more of a suspect?

He was dead now, though. He couldn't point fingers.

Except that was exactly what he was doing.

Didn't matter. I couldn't bring the blurs to reality. I couldn't if I wanted to stay sane. If I wanted to keep my life as I knew it.

I couldn't.

I cleared my throat. "Is there anything you can add, Ms. Romero?"

"That's pretty much it," she said. "May I go now?"

"Not quite yet," Charlie said.

I regarded her, the silver sparkle in her eyes laced with seriousness. "Do you have more questions?"

"Just one," Charlie said. "And it's a big one."

21

CHARLIE

Something about the Romero sisters didn't add up. I couldn't put my finger on it, but just being near Leta Romero made chills erupt on the back of my neck. I wasn't one to trust my intuition, but I did so now, without knowing exactly why.

"You've been honest about your sister. She values money."

"She does."

"Would you say she values it more than you do?"

"Why is that relevant?"

"Well, I'm assuming the Wolfes are paying you to be here. Am I correct?"

She reddened. "That doesn't mean—"

"Of course it does. It means you're willing to do something if it means you'll be paid. Does that also mean you're willing to throw your sister under a bus?"

"Charlie—" Roy began.

"This isn't a courtroom," I said. "She's here to answer our questions, and she's being paid to do so, right?"

He nodded. "Go ahead."

"I mean no disrespect, Ms. Romero. I'm just trying to get a

handle on your reasoning. Why in the world is this something you'd share with your gynecologist?"

"I don't know. You try thinking of something to say while your feet are in stirrups and a dude is looking between your legs."

"I've been there," I said. "Every woman has. And I don't think I'd be talking about a phone call my sister got about a billionaire's murder while I was being probed. Maybe it's just me."

Roy arched his brows and nodded slightly at me. I held back a smile. He liked where I was going, and Leta Romero was clearly uncomfortable.

"Here's the thing," I said. "Either you're making all of this up, and we can easily find that out by looking at your sister's cell phone records, or you're telling the truth, in which case there's got to be a reason you brought all of this up during a pelvic exam."

She reddened further.

Good. I'd struck a nerve.

"Can we speak to the doctor?" I asked Hoss.

"Manny? You can, I suppose. I can't guarantee he'll talk."

"He'll talk," Roy said.

Money. Roy would offer money, and Manny would talk.

"He's a friend of my brother's, and he doesn't want to see any of us implicated in this mess," Roy continued. "I'll make him an offer he can't refuse. He gave us *her* name, didn't he?" He nodded toward Leta Romero.

"Yeah, and I could have his medical license for that," Leta stated.

"You could, but I've paid you enough, and your attorney here"—he nodded to Hoss—"had you sign an agreement stating that you would not go after Manny's license in consideration of our payment to you."

She reddened again. Roy was telling the truth.

She was threatening her doctor's license? Granted, he'd given us her name, but only after talking to her first.

I had the feeling this apple didn't fall too far from the sister apple. Nieves might like money, and I was pretty sure Leta liked it just as much.

What I still couldn't quite wrap my head around, though, was the fact that she'd relayed all this information to Manny during a pelvic exam—an exam that clearly happened within days of the murder, between the time Rock left Montana and flew back a little over a week later with Lacey.

It all seemed too convenient.

"Ms. Romero consented to giving you an hour," Hoss said, standing. "The hour is now over."

Roy stood as well. "We appreciate your time. Both of you." He held out his hand first to Leta and then to Hoss.

I stood as well. "Yes, thank you both. We'll be in touch."

Should I have said that last part? That was Roy's place, not mine. Then again, I worked for the company. He didn't. Something that surprised me, after seeing him question Leta. He'd done a good job. Of course, Lacey had given him a written guide.

Lacey had often told me I had a good legal mind and that I should consider law school. Law school, though, meant college first. Seven years of my life. I was twenty-five now. I'd be thirty-two by the time I was done. Just didn't seem like a wise time investment. Not when my first love was art.

I could talk to Roy, but he'd hate the idea. He'd tell me to concentrate on my art. He'd also be talking from a trust fund perspective.

A girl had to make a living.

He smiled at me after Hoss and Leta had left the conference room. "I owe you a little something."

I recognized the look in his dark eyes.

He wanted me naked.

"Not here..." I said.

"Oh, yes. Here."

"But what if—"

"Who's going to walk in? I've paid for the use of this room for today. No one would dare."

"They might, if they saw our guests leave."

"Maybe someone will. If they do, I'll make sure they get a huge visual feast."

"Roy..."

"Come on, silver. All I could think about this last hour was having you on this table, sinking my tongue deep into your pussy and making your squirm and scream my name."

How could I argue with that? I was wet just listening to those words in that deep sexy timbre of his.

"Roy..." I said again.

"Charlie..." he echoed.

"Please..."

"Please what?"

Please stop. Please don't make me do this. Please, let's leave this room.

"Please," I said. "Please take me. Please."

22

ROY

This time I didn't worry about ruining her clothes. I'd buy her a new suit. I'd buy her a hundred suits. Better yet, I'd buy her clothes that fit her free spirit, her sparkling beauty, her artistic nature.

I yanked the blazer off her shoulders, letting it drop to the ground in a sticky tweed puddle.

Tweed had no place on Charlie Waters. If I had my way, she'd never wear it again.

Then the tweed skirt. Tweed? Covering up those treasures between her legs?

Never again.

Her blouse was better, a peach silk, and her hard nipples poked through. I brushed my fingers against one.

She groaned. "Yes, please."

"You like that? You like when I play with those sexy little nipples?"

Her answer was another groan.

They were delectable, and I lowered my head, taking one between my teeth right through her blouse and bra.

She bit her lip and inhaled sharply.

"It's okay," I said against the fabric of her blouse. "Scream if you want. Let it out. I dare anyone to open that door."

"Roy... Please..."

"I don't care. I don't care if the entire hotel management team comes in here, silver. I'm taking you. Right here. Right now." I bit the hard berry.

That got me the scream I'd been waiting for.

So I did it again.

I smiled against the swell of her breasts, the fabric of her blouse now wet from my mouth. God, she turned me on. Her body was still covered, and I was harder than I'd ever been.

Needed her. Needed her naked. Needed that naked nipple between my lips. Needed all of her.

I grabbed both sides of her blouse and ripped it open, the pearl buttons flying.

She gasped. "My blouse! I love this blouse!"

"I'll buy you five more." Then I attacked her bra. It was a front clasp, and I opened it with one maneuver, surprising myself. Her rosy breasts fell against her chest. Pure beauty.

Everything about her was pure beauty.

She was naked now, except for her businesslike black pumps and her white lacy panties. They were boy panties, pure white lace, and oh my God, they were hot.

I wished for a moment that I were an animal with sharp teeth and I could rip them off her and then attack what lay underneath.

I settled for yanking them off her beautiful ass, down her legs, and carefully easing them off her feet, leaving her pumps on.

Naked. Naked in black office girl pumps.

What a fucking feast.

I owed her an orgasm, and she was going to get it right on this mahogany table. The surface would be slick and shiny with something other than varnish when I was done with Charlie.

"Get on the table, silver. Sit down and spread those luscious legs for me."

She obeyed, wincing. "It's cold."

"Not for long. In a few minutes, you're going to be so hot you won't be able to contain yourself."

"I'm not doing a very good job of containing myself right now," she said. "I want to scream!"

"Then scream, honey. Scream your pretty little head off."

"I can't. I just can't."

"We'll see about that." I bent down, spreading her legs even farther apart. Man, she was bendy. And man, did that turn me on.

Her pussy was already ripe with nectar. Nectar sweeter than the juiciest peach. I inhaled for a moment, took in the spicy, musky scent of her. Of the woman who'd squirmed into my heart in less than three days.

Crazy.

Had any other woman smelled quite so enticing?

Granted, I hadn't been with many. Six, to be exact, and only one of them had lasted more than a couple days.

I hadn't thought about any of them in a long time. No one had responded to me the way my little silver did.

I wasn't sure anyone ever would again.

She squirmed beneath me. "Please. Please, Roy."

"I'm enjoying the view," I said naughtily.

"Can you enjoy it with your tongue in my pussy? Please?"

My cock strained against my jeans. Her voice had deepened a touch, and her words... God, her words...

"If you could see the sight before me, you'd understand. You're perfectly pink and swollen, and your clit is straining upward. And your scent. Like peaches and spice and musk. I can't get enough of it. Of looking at you and smelling you."

"If it smells that good, imagine how it must taste," she said breathlessly.

That did it. I clamped my mouth around her clit and sucked.

The orgasm came quickly, before I could tongue her or finger her. She'd been more ready than I even imagined, and God, it was fucking hot.

I nursed her through the orgasm, easing up on her clit as she wriggled beneath me. Her pussy lips pulsed against my chin as her climax continued.

"Keep going," I said against her flesh. "Give me more, silver."

Then I thrust two fingers inside her and sucked hard on her clit.

"Shit!" She pounded both fists on the wooden table, shrieking.

Yeah, that was what I was after. I wanted her to scream. I wanted everyone who walked by this room to hear her. To hear the shouts and pleasure of this amazing woman.

I nursed her through that orgasm and then another.

And another.

Until my cock couldn't take it any longer.

I stood and unzipped my jeans, sliding them over my hips. "I'm going to fuck you, silver. I'm going to sink my cock into you and make your scream even louder."

Her breasts were rosy and swollen, her nipples tight and hard.

I hadn't paid any attention to them since I'd freed them from her clothes, so before I shoved my cock into her, I gave them each a hard pinch.

She nearly jerked off the table.

"Good?" I said.

She bit her lip. "Do that again, and I'm going to scream so loud!"

"Good." I pinched those hard nipples once more.

She didn't disappoint. Her shrill shriek bounced off the walls of the conference room.

And I sank my cock deep into her wet pussy.

"Ahhhh," I groaned.

How perfectly she sheathed me. Paradise. Being inside Charlie Waters was true paradise.

"Play with my nipples while you fuck me, Roy. Please."

I clamped my hands onto her breasts as I pulled out and thrust back in. With my thumbs, I teased her, her vocal responses spurring me on and making me even harder, if that were possible.

I pumped.

I pumped.

Then I stayed deep inside her, moving my hips in a circular motion that touched every angle inside her cunt. She squirmed, her eyes closed, sexy moans easing out of her throat.

When I could no longer wait, I pulled out and plunged back in balls deep, releasing inside her warmth.

Every contraction of my cock emanated through me, from my very core to the tips of my fingers and toes. My fingers sizzled as I continued torturing her nipples.

"I'm coming, Roy. I'm coming again!"

A low groan left my throat. God, for her to come. For me to make her come.

That was almost better than my own release.

Something about bringing her to orgasm titillated me like nothing else.

I stayed embedded in her body for several timeless moments, letting my climax taper off slowly and completely.

When I finally came to, I was panting, breaths leaving my body in rapid puffs.

"Fuck," was all I could manage.

Charlie lay silently on the table, her body covered in a beautiful sheen of rosiness. Her nipples were still hard.

God, she was beautiful.

So fucking beautiful.

Finally I withdrew, and I smiled.

I'd promised this table would be shiny with her juices, and it was. Sheer, shiny beauty.

She dazzled. Everything about her fucking dazzled.

I tucked my cock back into my boxer briefs and put my jeans back over my hips.

Then I simply gazed at her beauty. Her nakedness. Her rosiness. And still wearing those businesslike pumps.

These weren't *fuck me* pumps.

They were simple black leather with a medium-high heel.

How great would she look in *fuck me* stiletto pumps?

Nope. Couldn't imagine that at the moment, or I'd get hard again.

She let out a slow sigh and a sweet vocal "mmm."

Then she jerked upward.

23

CHARLIE

"Oh my God!" I jerked upward, nearly sliding off the table. It was coated in...well...*me*.

How had I let this happen? I hadn't exactly been quiet. And Roy.

Roy had egged me on.

Where was his introversion today?

He eyed me like I was a side of prime beef. "You look succulent," he said.

"How could you let me do this?" I scanned the floor for my clothes. "People outside must have heard."

"So?"

"So?" I shook my head. "You're crazy, Roy. This is nuts."

"The Wolfes paid good money for this room."

"For God's sake, we have a suite upstairs. The Wolfes didn't pay for us to have sex in this room."

"The Wolfes paid for this room for the day. What we choose to do in it is our business."

I regarded him. For a split second, I'd thought he was different.

But no. He was Derek Wolfe spawn, through and through, just like Rock and Reid.

Reid was a known womanizer, and Rock? Well, I'd heard with my own ears what Rock was like when he and Lacey had fucked in her office that first day.

Crazy.

Roy, though? He had an artist's soul.

I stifled a chuckle.

Artists liked to fuck too, of course. Why wouldn't they?

I scrambled to find my clothes and get dressed.

My blouse was a huge issue. All of the buttons had been ripped off and scattered throughout the room. Now what was I supposed to do?

"Just put it on backwards and then put your blazer over it," Roy said, as if reading my mind. "No one will be the wiser."

I had to admit it was a good idea. Thankfully I had the sundress upstairs that I could change into.

I dressed as quickly as I could. "I need to go back to the room and change. I'm not going around wearing a backward blouse that isn't fastened at all in the back."

"Easier for me to get off that way."

"Right. You didn't have any trouble getting it off the first time."

"Silver, I'll never have any trouble getting you naked. I promise."

A sliver of anger surged through me. "Do you take any of this seriously? Do you?"

"Sure, I do. I take what we just did in here very seriously."

I punched his upper arm. "I'm not kidding."

"You think I am? That was some amazing sex, silver, and you know why? Because it was forbidden. We did it in a hotel conference room without a locked door—"

"That door was *unlocked?*" I nearly screamed.

He smiled. "It was. It *is*."

I rubbed my forehead. "Oh my God."

"It's no one's business."

"That's just it. This *is* business. I came here on business. On my third day of work. And I fucked the boss's brother in a hotel conference room. I'm history."

"You think *I'm* going to rat you out?"

"Not you. The manager. Anyone who walked by this room and heard what was so obviously going on in here."

"Like I said, it's no one's business. And if I know my brothers, they won't fire you for something they both would have done in a heartbeat."

I sighed. He was right about that. I'd been witness to one of them doing the same. Lacey could have easily been asked to leave her firm for that bout of unprofessionalism.

I respected Lacey more than anyone I knew. Never would I have expected...

I sighed again, regarding Roy. Silky strands of dark hair had come loose from his low ponytail. Sweat still beaded on his forehead.

He'd never looked sexier.

What was it about the Wolfe men?

They were gorgeous, no doubt. They were brilliant.

Yet I'd been around other gorgeous, brilliant men. I'd worked at a top Manhattan law firm, for goodness' sake.

No one had affected me like Roy Wolfe did.

Not even my ex, who was also gorgeous and brilliant.

But he wasn't Roy Wolfe.

No one was Roy Wolfe.

I'd made a complete spectacle of myself because I couldn't resist Roy Wolfe.

What the hell was happening to me?

I inhaled and then exhaled slowly. Time to walk out of this room with my head held high.

I couldn't help a laugh. Right. It would be obvious to anyone who saw us what we'd been up to. Roy looked lazily satisfied. And though I hadn't seen myself, I was pretty sure I was glowing with a "just fucked" look.

"For God's sake," I finally said. "Let's go."

AFTER AN EARLY DINNER at a local five-star eatery, Roy and I returned to the suite.

"We need to call Rock and Reid," he said. "Let them know how everything went."

I nodded. My belly was full. Dinner had been nice, and Roy and I had talked mostly about art. For a split second, I'd let myself forget about the real reason we were here.

All the Wolfes plus Lacey had been implicated in Derek Wolfe's murder.

Roy got his brothers on a conference call. I went to the bathroom to take a shower. It wasn't my place to horn in on the phone call unless I was asked to.

I showered quickly.

As much as I enjoyed our encounters, I didn't want Roy joining me this time. Why? I couldn't say. Yeah, I was a little embarrassed by our display earlier, but that wasn't the reason.

I was also as attracted to him as ever.

But as he sat talking on the phone with his brothers and Lacey, something bugged me.

I was putting my job in jeopardy. If I'd been representing Wolfe Enterprises today with anyone other than one of the Wolfe brothers, I'd be fired for what I'd done.

This hadn't been professional, and I was *always* professional.

Yeah, I'd asked Lacey if there was a problem with me dating Roy. I hadn't actually asked if it was okay if I had loud sex with him in a hotel conference room. Where anyone could hear. Or walk in, because the door hadn't been locked.

This had to stop.

And the only way it would stop was for me to stop seeing Roy.

The idea made my heart want to shatter into a thousand tiny shards. How could I give up the best sex I'd ever had with the most magnificent man I'd ever met? A man with a beautiful body and an artist's soul to match?

Still...Roy was not without issues. He was hiding something. I felt it in the marrow of my bones.

And the way he spoke of his sister... The naked envy in his tone. I couldn't blame him. He and his brothers had supposedly been treated terribly by their father while watching their baby sister be doted on as his favorite.

My head swung back to Leta Romero's words earlier.

Rock had said his sister was the reason he was sent away.

But his sister had been six then!

Still... the little girl was her father's favorite.

God, was he...? No, he couldn't have been abusing her. Reid and Roy would surely have known.

This puzzle had so many pieces, and none of them seemed to fit together.

I finished in the shower.

How the heck was I supposed to keep my distance from Roy when we were sharing a suite?

Easy enough. I'd retire to my bedroom and lock the door. I could do it now. I was already in here.

But that wouldn't be fair. I had to explain my reasoning to Roy.

I toweled off, moisturized all over, and then put on my shortie pajamas and clad myself in the lush white hotel robe. I inhaled deeply and opened the door, leaving my bedroom and entering the living area of the suite.

Roy was still on the phone with his brothers. He put his finger to his lips, motioning for me to be quiet. I nodded.

But I didn't leave. If he didn't want me there, he'd say so. I'd stay until he was done with his conversation, and then I'd talk to Roy about cooling things off.

Rock's voice: You sure that's what she said? What were her exact words?"

Roy: I can't recall her exact words, but Charlie took really good notes.

Rock: Is she there?

Roy: Yeah. Right here.

Rock: Get her on the line.

Roy nodded to me, and I grabbed the laptop out of my brief-case. I also grabbed my phone. I hadn't told Roy I recorded the conversation. Was now the time?

"Did you write down Leta's exact words about her conversations with Nieves?"

I smiled.

He cocked his head.

"I took good notes," I said, "and I also recorded the call."

Rock: You're a genius! No wonder Lace loves you so much.

Reid: Good call, Charlie.

Lacey: That's my girl.

Roy simply smiled and mouthed, "Nice."

"Can you play the recording for us?" Lacey asked.

"Yeah, of course. I was afraid you all would be angry at me for recording it."

"Of course not," Lacey said. "I was actually going to suggest you do so, but then I thought it might not be a very good idea. After all, it won't be admissible in court."

Rock: So what?

Reid: I'm with Rock. Thanks for thinking of it, Charlie.

I smiled to myself while Roy beamed at me. I pulled up the recording on my phone.

24

ROY

She was perfect. Perfectly beautiful, perfectly adorable, and perfectly brilliant. Who could ask for more in a woman?

I relived the conversation as the recording commenced.

When it was over, Reid spoke.

"What did she mean by that, Rock? Was she telling the truth? Did you tell her sister that Riley was the reason you were sent away?"

A cleared throat. Rock, I assumed. "I don't recall telling her that."

"Then she must have made it up," Reid said. "This was all a waste of time."

"The thing that bothers me," Lacey said, "is the same thing Charlie brought up. Why would she be talking to her gynecologist about this stuff? I've got to say, I've never told my gyn about any conversations I had with an old boyfriend. Any conversations I had period. It doesn't fly."

"Did she know you were acquainted with Manny, Rock?" Reid asked.

"Leta? I don't know," Rock said. "Nieves did. Nieves hung out with me on the weekends. We rode, and we often ran into Hoss and Manny."

"I meant Nieves," Reid said. "That's where this information allegedly comes from."

"You think Nieves—or rather, Leta—could have told Manny on purpose?" Lacey queried. "And this is after she got the phone call the night of Derek's murder."

"Pretty convenient, all told," Rock said. "But I sure can't see how it means anything with regard to the murder. I couldn't have done it. I wasn't in the state, so why talk about it at all with her doctor?"

"I agree," Lacey said, "in theory. But I also agree with Charlie that women don't normally discuss this kind of thing while some doctor is looking between their legs."

"Especially when that doctor is Manny," Rock said.

"What do you mean?" Lacey asked.

"You saw him. Would you let that guy salivate between your legs?"

"That's gross, Rock," Lacey said. "I'm sure he's a professional. But he is a little creepy."

"A lot creepy," Charlie added.

I thought of Charlie on the exam table, Manny's fat head between her legs.

Yeah. That would never happen.

But still something bit at my neck. My little sister. The sister Reid and I had envied because she had our father's attention.

He never beat on her. Only on us boys.

Did Rock feel the same way? Did he get angry because our father favored his only girl? Time for him to fess up.

"Is there any truth to it, Rock?" I asked. "Was Riley the reason you got sent away?"

A throat cleared, presumably Rock's.

"There's a story to tell," he said, "about what happened back then. I always felt it was Riley's and not mine."

"Things are getting real, here," Reid said. "We need to know all that you know."

A pause. Then, "You're right. We meet when Roy and Charlie return."

"Good enough," Reid agreed. "We should all be together. But what about Riley?"

"I'd like her there. Any word?"

"No," Reid said. "The best PIs in the business can't find her. I don't know who can."

"We'll fly home first thing tomorrow," I said.

"Good. Come straight to the office when you get here," Reid said. "We'll be waiting."

"All right. We done here?"

"Not quite," Reid said. "Terrence has set up Father Jim to do a memorial service."

Father Jim. The man who'd done my first communion. The man who...

Not going there. Can't. Not yet. The blurred images knocked on the door of my mind. Knocked loudly this time.

I didn't answer. *Couldn't* answer.

"Okay," Rock said. "When? Let's get this bullshit over with as soon as possible. We have real problems to deal with."

"Agreed," Reid said. "Terrence is getting the word out. It'll be next week. Wednesday at two p.m. at St. Andrew's."

"Because Dad was such a good churchgoer," Rock scoffed.

"Dad donated a shit ton of money to that parish," Reid said. "Father Jim owes us. Plus, having it at a church will make it look better to the public."

"And a wake afterward, I suppose?" I said.

"Of course. Derek Wolfe style."

"A fuck ton of cash," Rock complained.

"We have it. We won't even notice it's gone," Reid said.

"Still..."

I agreed with my older brother. Money wasted as far as I was concerned. As far as we all were concerned. I was ready for this conversation to end.

"Is that it?" I asked.

"I think so," Rock said, an edge to his voice I hadn't heard before.

"Okay. Bye then." I ended the call.

I turned to Charlie.

She was sex on a stick in that robe, her hair freshly washed and wet. Normally I'd be all over her.

But something niggled at me.

Rock had been keeping a secret.

Something about Riley.

He wasn't the only one with a secret.

Those undefined images whirled in my mind. I hadn't let myself see them in so long.

But if Rock was going to show us what he'd been hiding...

I should do the same.

I hadn't let myself think about that time clearly in over a decade.

For so long, I'd kept it a blur, let it fuck with my mind but stay out of my life.

Oh, it came out. It came out in my art, particularly in the abstract in the lobby of the Wolfe building—the painting that had brought me to Charlie.

The painting that had tortured my soul to complete, but that, to this day, was my best work.

I'd had offers in the seven figures for it, offers I'd never had before for anything I'd painted.

I'd turned down every single one of them.

Every. Single. One.

That painting was too personal. Locked inside it was a truth I couldn't yet acknowledge.

And I didn't paint a key.

25

CHARLIE

B ack at the office the next day, I dived into my work. Anything to get my mind off Roy Wolfe.

Oddly, he hadn't balked when I refused to sleep with him last night. I'd expected a fight. Honestly, I'd expected I'd give in.

Even though I knew it was for the best until I knew him better, I was disappointed he'd acquiesced so easily.

Something was bothering him.

Lacey asked me to help Terrence put the memorial service for Derek Wolfe together. We had five days to plan a first-class service that showed the world how much the Wolfe siblings missed their father.

Big problem number one—one of said siblings had disappeared.

Big problem number two—the other three hated him.

Money was no object, I'd been told. Plan the most elaborate service and hang the costs.

So I would.

Roy would be in the office later. The siblings and Lacey were meeting to discuss what Rock had to tell them about Riley. I hadn't been included in that, which was just as well. First, I wasn't family. Second, I didn't particularly want to see Roy.

We'd both be better off away from each other until I figured him out a little better and he stopped hiding whatever he was hiding.

Leta Romero also never left my mind. Someone had made that phone call to her sister an hour before Derek was actually murdered.

Was it possible the cops got the time of the murder wrong? Not likely.

I sighed. Better not to dwell on Leta or anything else. I had work to do.

Terrence had given me a bunch of numbers to call for catering for the wake after the service. The wake would be held at the Waldorf Astoria, with limos transporting guests from St. Andrew's.

The Wolfes were spending a crazy amount of money.

A crazy amount of money to make it look like they were mourning their bastard father.

Of course, it was pennies to them.

I shook my head. I couldn't even comprehend the amount of money in the Wolfe coffers. When you got into billions, did numbers even matter anymore?

Damn.

My phone buzzed.

"Charlie Waters," I said into my Bluetooth.

"Charlie, hello."

Blaine Foster. I could tell by his voice, of course, but more so how he said "hello." It came out more like "hell-oo."

"Blaine, what can I do for you?"

"Just checking in. How's the new job?"

"It's good, thank you."

"And Lacey?"

"She's fine. Doing well."

"It's not every day a lawyer becomes personal counsel to the CEO of a billion-dollar enterprise. And so quickly too."

"You know as well as I do how she got the position, Blaine."

"True. I always thought highly of Lacey. Smart as a whip, that one."

"Yes, she is."

"Or was, anyway."

"What's that supposed to mean?"

"She married a man she's known for less than a month."

"They fell in love. And why the hell am I explaining this to you?"

"You certainly don't owe me any explanation."

"You're right about that. Thank you for calling, Blaine, and checking in. I'm doing great."

"How about lunch today?"

Seriously? We were so over. "I don't think so."

"Reconsider."

"Uh...no, I won't reconsider. Goodbye, Blaine."

"Charlie—"

"What? What is it? I'm knee deep into planning a billionaire's memorial service. I don't have time to argue with you."

"Reconsider. I have information you might need."

BLAINE FOSTER WAS STILL a silver fox with abs that could kill. Not that I could see them past his Armani elegance, but I knew what lay beneath that cotton button-down and wifebeater. The man was in his late fifties, but damn, his abs could cut ice.

He ordered for both of us, which irked me. It hadn't bothered me when we were dating, but now? I found it patronizing. Roy never did that.

Wait. I'd never actually been out on a date with Roy. I had no idea whether he'd order for me.

Big lightbulb moment.

Blaine was one of the middle-aged professional men who had a *first wife* and *first kids*. I'd seen it before, while working at the firm. A man married young, right out of law school, and had children. Then he became successful and began catching the eyes of younger ladies.

Yeah, I'd fallen into that trap. I hadn't caused his divorce, but I was certain someone in my age bracket had.

The man would then divorce *first wife* when *first kids* were in high school, marry *second wife*, have a vasectomy reversal, and start *second family*.

It was kind of sickening.

Of course *first wife* would ride the alimony pony and get child support until *first kids* turned eighteen. Maybe longer, if Dad was willing to pay for their college.

But usually Dad was focused on younger, hotter wife and *second kids* by then. *First kids* got the shaft.

I knew.

I was a *first kid*.

A big reason why I didn't go to college was because my father had a new family to support. Apparently college wasn't important for his *first kid*, and I didn't want to go into major debt. My mother would have helped all she could, but all she could wasn't enough.

So no college education for me.

Although Derek Wolfe had divorced his first wife, he hadn't remarried and had a bunch of new kids. The Wolfes could at least be thankful for that.

"What did you want to tell me?" I asked Blaine. Might as well get right to the point.

"You look beautiful, Charlie."

I stopped myself from rolling my eyes. Yeah, he was still looking for *second wife* material. That was why he'd gotten too serious on me too quickly.

I still wasn't going to bite.

Yes, he was attractive. Yes, he was brilliant. Yes, he had a lot of money.

If that hadn't swayed me before, it certainly wouldn't now.

He was no Roy Wolfe.

Not that I *had* Roy Wolfe. I wasn't sure where we stood at the moment.

"What did you want to tell me, Blaine?"

"What? No response to me telling you how stunning you are?"

"Thank you. Now, what did you want to tell me?"

"How about, 'You look great too, Blaine.'"

I set my water glass down on the table a bit more harshly than I'd intended. "You always look great. You know that. You don't need me to stroke your ego. Go look in a mirror, for God's sake."

Blaine took a sip of his cabernet. He always drank at lunch, another thing that bothered me about him. His clients paid him seven hundred and fifty dollars an hour. He should be free of alcohol when he did their work.

"I'm not sure what I've done to produce such obstinance in you."

Yet another thing that irked the hell out of me. He treated me like a child. To him, I *was* a child. We were over thirty years apart.

I smiled sweetly, though forced. "If you have something you think I need to know, please just tell me."

"I will. I have every intention to, but first, can we just enjoy each other's company for a few minutes?"

"Look, Blaine—"

"I've missed you, Charlie."

"I've been gone from the firm for less than a week," I reminded him.

"It's not that, so much, though it was nice to see your pretty face daily. It's more...I miss what could have been between us."

I don't. I couldn't exactly say that, though, or he might not give me the information he thought I needed.

Which of course could be nonexistent. It might have been a ploy to get me to lunch.

"We've been through this," I said. "You were moving too fast for me. I'm so much younger. I'm not ready for something so permanent."

"I'm willing to slow down."

No, you're not. You're looking for second wife. I know your story.

Of course those words didn't leave the back of my throat.

Because it didn't matter. Not now.

"I'm sorry. I've met someone else."

He wrinkled his forehead. "So soon?"

"Blaine, you went out with Alice Engle two days after we broke up."

"That? I was mentoring her."

This time I let my eyeroll through. "Not buying it. Sorry."

"I'm serious. She's a law clerk. You know that."

"She's also my age. And gorgeous. And smart. Just your type."

He opened his mouth, but I gestured him to stop.

"Please, Blaine. I can't date you anymore. I hope that doesn't keep you from giving me whatever information you have that you think I need."

26

ROY

I f nausea had an image, it would be the one in my mind right now.

My baby sister, six years old, my sick father hovering over her, touching her.

Hurting her.

Rock, my brother I hardly knew—the man with the hardest exterior I'd ever seen—had been reduced to a few tears while telling the story.

He'd gone out of his head at fourteen, when testosterone was raging through his body, urging him to take risks, when his brain didn't let him see past tomorrow.

He'd gone after the bastard with a knife.

I didn't know whether to be frightened of my brother or to applaud him.

In reality, I felt both.

But that had been adolescent Rock. The Rock of today, other than an arrest for a biker brawl he hadn't started, had kept his nose clean.

He didn't speak highly of Buffington Academy, the military school our father had sent him to. I could only imagine what he'd gone through there. Of course, it was probably better than juvenile hall, where he would have gone if my parents had pressed charges.

All those years...

Reid and I locked gazes.

"God. Riley," Reid said, his eyes glassy. "We always thought she was his favorite."

"He took her on all those special trips." I gulped back the breakfast that threatened to emerge on the table in front of me.

"My room was next to hers," Rock said absently. "There was no way either of you could know."

"Still," I said. "How could we have been so blind? So envious of everything he lavished on her?"

"We need to find her," Reid said. "Get her the help she needs."

"Except she doesn't want to be found," Rock said. "The two of you have told me that more than once."

"But she needs—"

"Look," Rock continued, "I'm not in her shoes, but I do know what it's like to be thrust into a situation over which you have no control. I'm not going to lie to you and say I'm completely over all of it, but I tell you. The big sky of Montana did a lot to heal me. I had to let it go and accept that I couldn't save her. I'd tried, but I couldn't. He would never let me. Being away from all this dysfunction did a lot to heal me. Why do you think I was so damned angry when the bastard made me come back here to run his company? And if I didn't, all of you would pay? What the fuck kind of thing is that to do to your kid?" He shook his head.

"We were all surprised by it," Reid said, "and frankly, now I'm even more confused. If you truly tried to do him in—"

"I was fourteen. I was hotheaded. I never would have been successful, in retrospect. But damn, there are times I still wish I had been. All of you could have been spared what you went through."

"We didn't go through what Riley went through," I said.

"No," Reid agreed, "we didn't. He didn't touch us sexually. But we did go through a lot. You, not as much, Roy, because you kept to yourself. But he used me for a punching bag on a regular basis. I was the target once you left, Rock."

"I'm sorry," Rock said.

"You were fourteen, like you said. You didn't think it through. But that was the end result."

"I got whaled on my fair share," I said. "I won't pretend he was as hard on me as he was on you, Reid, but it's not like I got off scot-free."

I well remembered taking the insufferable beatings from my father.

"How long did the physical abuse go on?" Rock asked.

"Until we were big enough to stop it," Reid replied.

Silence.

For the first time in my life, sitting here with Rock and Reid, I truly felt like we were brothers. Brothers that went beyond DNA. Brothers who understood each other. Brothers of the soul.

We were all completely different people, but we were connected by more than our blood.

"It's pretty clear," Reid said, "why Riley disappears every now and again."

"Most interesting is that she did the disappearing act before our father was murdered," Rock said. "Was he around when she wasn't?"

Reid gulped audibly.

Was he?

I looked to Reid. "I stayed away from him, and I was never in the office. I have no idea if he was around when she wasn't."

"I guess I never thought much about it," Reid said. "I was

always in the office, but I steered clear of him as much as I could. I mean, who wouldn't?"

"She's gone now," Rock said, "and we know she's not with him. I think it's safe to assume it's possible she wasn't with him when she disappeared before."

"Who knows what we can assume at this point?" Reid said.

I nodded.

After what Riley had been through at our father's hands, of course she wanted to disappear. Hell, I'd thought about it more than once. And Rock? He'd done it. After military school, he'd never returned to Manhattan.

Now, having been to Montana twice, I understood why.

Montana was good for a person's soul. It was almost a cleansing balm.

I needed to cleanse myself before I could be with Charlie again. She deserved a whole man, not someone whose insides were as big a mess as mine were.

God, the secrecy.

Rock had spilled his biggest secret.

Now I had to spill mine.

Except I'd held it in for so long—hidden it from even myself —that I wasn't sure I could put it into words.

"Father Jim," was all I said.

"What about him?" Reid asked.

"I don't want him doing the memorial service."

"Why not? Dad gave that church a ton of money over the years. He owes us."

"It's not that."

"Wait," Reid said. "We used to make jokes about the altar boys going into the confessional with Father Jim, but are you saying..."

I shook my head vehemently. "No. He never touched me. Never touched any kid, that I know of."

"Then what's the beef with him?" Rock said.

Indeed, what *was* the beef with him?

I'd suppressed everything for so long. So, so long.

Was Father Jim in those blurred images? Or wasn't he?

"Nothing," I said.

Rock cleared his throat. "I don't buy it. What's the problem with Father Jim?"

"Dad wasn't a religious man."

"So what?"

"We shouldn't have a priest doing his service. That's all."

Yeah, that was all.

Nothing more there.

Except it was a lie.

I knew something about Father Jim. Something I couldn't put into words yet. It had nothing to do with the altar boys or the nuns. Or even the parishioners.

No, it was far more sinister.

It concerned my father.

And I'd buried it long ago.

For good.

27

CHARLIE

"Of course not," Blaine said. "That's the reason I invited you to lunch."

Right. The other stuff was just to soothe his own ego. He didn't want me back any more than I wanted him back. Which was fine with me.

"Then what is it?" I asked.

"It's about Derek Wolfe."

"Okay. What about him?"

"Don't you think it's strange there hasn't been a funeral yet?"

"Not particularly. They're planning it now. It'll be next week."

"I see. I'll look forward to it."

"You're coming?"

"Of course. Derek and I go way back. He was our firm's biggest client."

Right. That was how Lacey had gotten involved in all this.

"I understand the police are investigating all of his children...and Lacey."

I dropped my mouth open. I didn't know why I was

surprised. It must be common knowledge. A high-profile billionaire had been murdered.

"Yes. They're all innocent."

"I believe they probably are."

"Does this have something to do with what you want to tell me?"

"Yeah, actually. I like Lacey. Always have. I don't for a minute believe she could murder anyone, not even Derek Wolfe."

"Good. Because she didn't. And you're right. She doesn't have it in her."

"As for the Wolfe siblings, I don't know them well, other than Reid. Reid shares his father's business acumen, and he's a pretty nice guy. Derek Wolfe paid our firm a lot of money over the years, so we did our share of ass kissing. But I'll be honest with you, Charlie."

I nodded.

"He *wasn't* a nice guy."

Right. Tell me something I don't know.

"Uh-huh," was all I said.

"I'm not sure what Lacey thought of him, but she hadn't worked with him very long. He could be very charming when he wanted to be."

"Lacey doesn't discuss her clients with me," I said.

"Charlie, of course she does. You're her assistant."

"She would never say anything disrespectful about a client."

"That's to her credit, then." He cleared his throat when the waiter came by with our food.

Lasagna Bolognese. His favorite. I'd told him once that I loved it as well—which was true—and he'd apparently taken that to mean I wanted to eat nothing else. He ordered it for me whenever we went to a place that served it.

"Sure you don't want a glass of wine?" He touched his finger to his goblet, indicating to the waiter to bring him another.

"I don't drink during the workday."

He laughed. "You're young yet."

I didn't reply. It was easier not to. A petty argument over day drinking wasn't the reason I was here. I wanted the information he said he had for me.

I took a small bite of my lasagna, chewed, and swallowed. Then a large gulp of my iced tea. "So Derek Wolfe wasn't a nice guy. That's kind of common knowledge, Blaine."

"He's a tiger in the boardroom, yes," Blaine said. "I'm talking about personally."

"Oh?"

This still wasn't news to me. Did he really think I was that ignorant?"

"Yes. Let me tell you again. I don't for a minute believe Lacey had anything to do with Wolfe's murder. That's why I want to give you this information."

"Okay. Please do, then." I took another bite of food.

"About six years ago, I took a case for Derek Wolfe. It was under the table, and he paid me in cash. At his request, I destroyed all the records pertaining to the case."

I gulped. "What kind of case?"

"It had the potential to be a criminal case. A big criminal case. But we kept it out of the cops' hands. It cost Wolfe plenty, let me tell you."

"Quit beating around the bush, Blaine."

"There's one problem," he said.

"What's that?"

"Attorney-client privilege."

"That died with Derek, didn't it?"

"No, not generally. There's still the issue of ethical confidentiality. But Derek's not the problem. There was another client in the case, and he's still very much alive."

I sighed. "Look, Blaine. If you've destroyed the file, all we have is you."

"Not true. There's the victim."

"And you're willing to tell me who that is?"

"I'm not willing to tell you who she is. But Lacey knows the name. That's all I can say."

"Are you saying Lacey worked on the case?"

"I'm not saying anything of the sort. Lacey's a trusts-and-estates attorney."

"Then how on earth—" I stopped talking when the waiter came by to refill Blaine's wine.

Then I lowered my voice. "How on earth would she know the victim?"

"Apparently the signature page of our confidential settlement agreement was inadvertently left in the copy room by a secretary who was subsequently and immediately fired. Lacey was a young attorney and was working late. She found it on the floor of the copy room and brought it to me the next day. Luckily, only the victim's name was on the page. Nothing about why we were entering into a settlement with her."

"Was Derek Wolfe's name on the page?"

"Yes."

"And the other client's?"

He nodded.

"But nothing about the situation."

"No. Like I said, it was the signature page."

"I see. What did you tell Lacey?"

"I thanked her for her discretion and asked that she not mention it to anyone. She was a young associate at the time, so of course she agreed."

"What are the chances she'd remember a name she saw on the signature page of a document years ago?"

"Since it's Lacey, I'd say the chances are good."

"Even so, how would that do us any good? What if it's a common name, like Lisa Smith or something. How would that help?"

"I see your point. You always were a smart one, Charlie."

"Spare me your backhanded compliments. Please just answer the question, Blaine."

He smiled. "You're still as feisty as ever. I can have a hotel room booked in five minutes, babe. You're driving me insane."

"You're drunk."

"On two glasses of wine?"

"No. I'm betting you had a drink before our lunch."

He smiled again. "Like I said, you're a smart girl."

Woman, but whatever. It wasn't worth arguing over. "We've been through this a million times. We want different things."

"I'm not talking about a relationship. I'm talking about some afternoon delight. We never had a problem in that department."

No, we hadn't—other than his distaste for cunnilingus—but now that I'd been with Roy Wolfe? Blaine Foster was a piss-poor substitute.

"Can we get back to the subject, please?"

"You'll change your mind eventually."

"I won't today. Please, Blaine? This is important. Lacey's well-being depends on it."

He softened then. He truly had been fond of Lacey. "I can't give you the name, but I can tell you this. It wasn't a common name like Lisa Smith. Bob Mayes always said Lacey had a memory like he'd never seen. Photographic. Ask her. She'll remember."

28

ROY

"I don't give a rat's ass who does the service," Rock said.

"Then you're overruled, Roy," Reid said. "Father Jim it is."

I lost that battle. So what? I'd suppressed the stuff for so long. Did it really matter?

"What about Riley?" I asked.

"Riley's not here."

"That's not what I mean. Now that we know what our father did to her, shouldn't we step up our efforts to find her?"

"We can't step it up more than we already have," Reid said. "We've always had the best PIs on it. She doesn't want to be found."

My stomach hurt. Not nauseating hurt, though nausea overwhelmed me also.

No. This was a bloody hurt, a sharpness. A feeling of impending doom.

"Are we done here?" I asked.

"Have you told us everything, Rock?" Reid asked.

"Everything about why I was sent to Buffington, yeah."

"Is there anything else?"

"Only what I went through at that hellhole. It fucked me up. But it made me stronger."

"Hazing?" Reid asked.

Rock only nodded. "I won't go into the gory detail. Luckily I escaped most of it because I was big enough at fourteen. But three years later, I was expected to do the same to others."

I gulped. "Did you?"

"I'm not proud of the monster I became, but my abuse was only verbal and physical. I refused to..." He shook his head.

"Wow," Reid said. "I'm sorry, Rock. I used to blame you."

"For what?" Rock bellowed.

"You already know. When you left, Dad needed a new punching bag. Roy was a recluse, hardly ever around. So it was me."

"I got my fair share," I added.

"You did. I'm not taking away from that, but I got the brunt of it."

I couldn't deny it. Reid was correct. "You mouthed off a lot more," I said.

That got a smile out of Rock. "Really? Hard to imagine."

"I learned from you," Reid said to Rock.

"I'm sorry, little brother," Rock said. "My only excuse is that I was fourteen and I didn't consider the consequences."

"Not blaming you," Reid said. "Not anymore. I was a kid. But not now, and especially now that we know what really happened."

A knock on the door interrupted us.

"Yeah?" Rock said. "Come in."

Lacey walked in.

"Hey, babe." Rock raised his eyebrows.

"Sorry to interrupt."

"It's okay. We're all done here. What do you need?"

"Charlie just called. She had lunch with a former partner of mine, and he gave her some information she thinks might help us with the situation with your father. She didn't want to discuss it over the phone, but she's on her way back. She wants to see all of us."

All of us? I didn't actually work here, like the others. I wasn't sure I could handle myself around Charlie.

I hadn't fought her when she didn't want to sleep with me last night.

And now?

God, I was fucked up.

"When will she be here?"

Then another knock.

Lacey opened the door. "Looks like she's here now."

HER VOICE WAS like an angel's. Her body sculpted by gods. Her hair like waves of grain blowing in the breeze.

I could hardly focus on Charlie's words.

Something about a confidential settlement.

A woman with an unusual name.

Derek Wolfe...and someone else.

"Wow," Lacey said, interrupting my thoughts. "I remember that."

"Blaine seemed sure you'd remember the woman's name."

"I was a brand new associate," Lacey said, "and a senior partner told me to basically forget I'd ever seen it."

"You can do it, baby," Rock said.

"Did he give you any other information?" she asked Charlie.

Charlie shook her head. "Just that he couldn't say any more because the other client in the settlement is still alive."

Lacey widened her eyes. "Usually my memory is a curse. Now, when I need it, I can't bring it to the surface."

"Maybe try some guided hypnosis," Reid said.

Rock scoffed. "What kind of crap are you talking about?"

"It's not crap. It's a type of therapy."

"You ever tried it?"

"No, but I've read about it."

"You read about therapy techniques?"

"For God's sake, Rock," Reid said, "there's more to me than a business head. Sometimes I actually read something else."

"*Psychology Today?*"

My brothers continued to bat their metaphorical ball back and forth.

I concentrated on Charlie. She looked more beautiful than ever, even in her starchy blue suit. She was a little more casual today, pants instead of a skirt. A shame to cover those legs, though.

Those milky legs that had wrapped around me...

"Roy!"

I jerked in surprise. "What?"

"Are you even listening?" Reid asked.

"Yeah. Woman with a strange name. Guided hypnosis."

"Do you know anything about it?" Rock asked.

"About what? Guided hypnosis?"

"Uh...yeah. That's what we're talking about. That's what I asked you."

"Why would I know anything?"

"I guess that's a no," Reid said.

"Why would I know anything about it?" I asked again.

"Just a question, Roy," Rock said. "Chill out."

Did my brothers really think I'd been in therapy? Did Charlie think I had?

I wanted a hole to open up in the ground so it could swallow me up.

What made them think...?

Did they know something?

Know something was hidden deep within me?

Shit. I was making things up.

Guided hypnosis, though...

Those blurred images that I couldn't bring to the surface...

Could guided hypnosis help?

Because there was something locked away in my mind, something hidden so deep I couldn't access it. Couldn't...

Or didn't want to...

But it was there, and it was important. Important to what we were trying to accomplish.

God, I didn't want to go there.

But it was time.

I had to.

Perhaps it would be a relief from the constant mindfuck.

I needed to know more about this guided hypnosis.

"I'll keep thinking on it," Lacey said. "Maybe I'll try the hypnosis thing. Do you know anyone who's any good, Reid?"

My brother shook his head. "Just read an article."

She turned to Charlie. "Find me a therapist in the area. Let's get this figured out."

"Will do." Charlie stood. "Anything else?"

"Not that I can think of," Lacey said. "Guys?"

Reid and Rock shook their heads. Charlie looked to me.

"I don't work here," was all I said.

"This concerns you as much as the rest of us," Rock said.

"What I meant was, I don't work here, so I can't give Charlie orders."

Charlie regarded me, her eyes slightly...sad?

Shit. Now I'd done it. But how? I was being respectful, not ordering her around. Right?

I held back a sigh. I'd never understand women.

29

CHARLIE

"What's bothering you?" Lacey asked, strolling into my office.

Your brother-in-law.

But I wasn't about to say that. Lacey had told me that getting involved with Roy wouldn't be a problem as far as she was concerned, so I certainly wasn't about to tell her I was upset about him. I refused to make it a problem.

"Nothing. I'm good."

"We've been working together for a couple years, Charlie. I know when something's bothering you."

"It's Blaine," I lied. "He wants to start things up again."

"Ah." Lacey smiled.

"I'm not interested."

"I can see why."

I raised my eyebrows.

"I mean...you and Roy."

Apparently she was intent on talking about it. "Roy and I aren't an item."

"Even after the luxurious trip on the jet?"

I chuckled. "We didn't join the mile-high club, if that's what you're wondering."

She laughed then. "Rock and I didn't, either."

My eyebrows nearly flew off my forehead.

"That surprises you?"

Yeah, it did, given their tryst in her office the first time they met, but I didn't want Lacey to know I'd heard them.

"Just...Rock seems..." My cheeks warmed. "None of my business, Lace. Sorry."

"Don't give up on Roy."

"I promise you that anything that happens with Roy won't interfere with my work here."

"I know it won't, and that's not what I meant. I just meant... there's something about Roy. Something special. I can't quite put my finger on it."

"He's hiding something," I blurted out.

This time *her* eyebrows took flight. "He is?"

"Yeah. I mean, I don't know for sure. I suppose it's just a feeling. Something I sense in him. Something I see in his art, too."

"How well do you know him, Charlie?"

"Not well. Only in the biblical sense."

She smiled.

"I didn't mean to say that. It kind of just popped out."

"All the Wolfe men are gorgeous," Lacey said. "But there's something special about Roy. Something almost...angelic."

"His long hair?" I said, though that wasn't it. I knew what she meant. It wasn't angelic. It was a weird sort of innocence that had been tainted.

"Maybe the hair is part of it," Lacey said.

"Probably it's the fact that he's an artist," I said. "He's kind of a closed book on the outside, but then you look at his artwork, and you realize there's so much inside him just clawing to get out."

Lacey nodded. "You've given this a lot of thought."

"I enjoy art, mainly, and I see some darkness in his. Don't get me wrong. He's an incredible talent, and his work is amazing."

"I don't know anything about art," she said, "so I'll take your word for it. I do think his work is beautiful."

"It is. He has a beautiful soul."

I suppressed a groan. Had I really just said that to my boss?

"Like I said, don't give up on him. If he's anything like his brother, he'll be a tough nut to crack. But the reward will be all the sweeter." She smiled and left my office.

Hmm. I definitely hadn't cracked Roy Wolfe. Did I want to? Did I want to be a part of whatever he was hiding?

Did I want to be a part of that darkness?

The night sky was dark, and the most beautiful stars shone only against the black veil of night.

Perhaps Roy was like a star, shining most brightly in darkness.

Or perhaps I was simply starstruck.

This was getting ridiculous.

I had a job to do, and the Wolfes were paying me a ridiculous amount of money to do it.

Lacey had asked me to find a therapist who specialized in guided hypnosis, so that was what I'd do.

30

ROY

I stood in front of Charlie's door, my fist suspended in midair, ready to knock.

What was stopping me?

She was researching guided hypnosis therapists. I needed one.

I also needed her.

My fist came down on the wooden door lightly.

"Yes?" came through the door. "Who is it?"

"It's me. Roy."

A pause. Then, "Come in."

I opened the door and walked in. Charlie sat at her desk, a pencil tucked behind one ear, papers scattered in front of her.

"What can I do for you?" she asked.

So professional. So polite.

So "we haven't had the hottest sex ever."

So strange.

"I was wondering..."

If you'd share the information about guided hypnosis, I finished in my mind.

Instead, what came out was, "if you'd like to have dinner tonight."

She paused, biting her lower lip. "I have a lot of work to do. I should probably stay late."

"A late dinner, then?"

Yeah, I wanted the name of the therapist.

But I wanted dinner with Charlie more. Just looking at her, I could feel the intense chemistry between us sizzling.

My dick responded, as it always did when Charlie was around.

She sighed. "Sure. Let's have dinner. We should talk."

Talk? That was never good. She was the one who'd said she didn't want to spend the night together at the hotel. Of course, I hadn't argued the point either.

"Charlie?"

I turned. A large man with silvery hair stood in her office doorway.

"Blaine? What are you doing here?"

Blaine Foster. The partner at Lacey's firm who Charlie'd had lunch with.

"Just came by to see Lacey."

"About what we discussed earlier?"

He cleared his throat. "Yes, actually." He nodded toward me. "Could you excuse us, please, Mr. Wolfe?"

"He knows everything you told me," Charlie said. "He can stay."

"I'm not here on business," he said.

"Then I'm definitely staying." I smiled and took a seat.

"Roy..." Charlie began.

"Is there something going on I should know about?" Blaine asked.

"Nothing that's any of your business," I replied.

"Okay, then." He cleared his throat again. "How about dinner?"

"Love to," I said sarcastically.

"He was talking to me, Roy."

I simply smiled.

"I already have plans," Charlie said.

"Change them."

I stood. "They're with me."

"You? Roy 'pretty boy' Wolfe?"

I cocked my head. "Pretty boy? This pretty boy would be happy to slam your head through the wall."

Charlie stood then. "Blaine, please leave. Unless you have more information for me—"

"Maybe I do."

"Then you can tell me here. Now. No need for you to spend your money on another meal for me."

"Maybe I like your company."

Then I saw it. That look in his eyes.

He'd slept with Charlie.

My Charlie.

I lowered my eyelids slightly and clenched my jaw. "Get out," I said.

"Is this your office, Mr. Wolfe?"

"It's my *company*," I said.

"Last I heard, it's your brother's company. You don't even have a position here."

Charlie moved from behind her desk and positioned herself between us. "Stop it, both of you. Blaine, I'm having dinner with Roy tonight. Sorry, he asked first. If you have information—"

"Never mind," Blaine said. "I'm done here."

"Good," I said through my clenched teeth, after he'd left and closed the door.

"Thanks a lot," Charlie said. "Now I'll never get whatever information he had."

"He didn't have any information."

"And how do you think you know that?"

"He wanted to fuck you, Charlie."

Her cheeks reddened. "I assure you—"

"Don't even try. I could see it. You and he were together."

"For a little while. I ended it."

"Why? A big partner in a successful law firm? He'd be a catch. Of course, a Wolfe would be a much better catch."

She huffed, her hands whipping to her hips. "Get out."

"Sorry. I own this building."

"You're ridiculous. If you think for one minute that I was interested in either Blaine *or* you because of money, you don't know me at all."

Yeah. I was a jerk. A first-class douche.

"Our dinner date, then? What time should I pick you up?"

"I'm *not* going to dinner with you."

I sat down. "I'm sorry."

Her eyes widened. "What?"

"I said I'm sorry."

I was. I'd been a jerk for no reason.

"Uh...okay."

"So then...dinner?"

"Roy..."

"Come on. I said I was sorry, and I need to talk to you about some stuff."

"What stuff?"

"Dinner, okay?"

She sighed. "All right. But I'll meet you there. I'm going to be working until the last minute."

"All right. I'll email you the details." I stood. "See you later."

31

CHARLIE

Eight o'clock at the Red Room.

I was hardly dressed for the Red Room. The place reeked of cocktail dresses. Here I was in my crisp linen suit. Navy blue, the professional color. A power suit, career counselors called it. Yeah, I'd gone to a career counselor after high school, since I couldn't afford college without going into major debt. I got no help from my father, who was busy with *second kids*. And my mother was a marketing assistant, which created another dilemma. She earned too much for me to qualify for any financial aid other than loans, but not enough to actually afford to pay for tuition.

Them's the breaks, as my high school guidance counselor had said.

Yeah, he really said that, bad grammar and all.

The career counselor had steered me to an inexpensive— well, inexpensive compared to college. I still had to take a small loan—paralegal course of studies at the local community college, one of the few that didn't require a college degree. I had great grades, so the counselor helped me get in.

Blaine had once called me a workaholic.

Seriously. A senior partner in a Manhattan law firm had called me, Charlie Waters, who didn't have a college degree, a workaholic.

I wasn't a workaholic, but I did have a work ethic. My mother might not have been able to afford to send me to college, but she did teach me the value of working hard and doing the best job possible.

But was there any truth in Blaine's words?

I truly had worked up until I had to leave to meet Roy. But could those last-minute things have waited until morning?

Being dressed a little nicer would have made a nice statement.

Power suits might be professional, but they were blah.

Uncomfortable and blah.

"I'm meeting someone here," I said to the maître d'. "Roy Wolfe."

"Yes, Mr. Wolfe has already arrived. Let me show you to his table."

His table. Not *your* table. As if Roy was the important one, and I was nothing more than his arm candy for the evening.

As I glanced around the posh restaurant, I saw that most of this evening's arm candy were dressed a lot better than I was.

Oh, well. He knew I'd be coming straight from work.

Roy stood as I approached the table.

God, could he be any sexier? His hair was in his signature slicked-back low ponytail, and he wore a navy-blue suit and tie.

Yes, a tie!

I'd never seen him wear one. The Red Room must have required it. I couldn't imagine him wearing that noose around his neck for any other reason.

The navy-blue suit, though. He'd seen what I was wearing, slacks and all. Had he worn basically the same thing on purpose? We looked like the Bobbsey twins on career day.

"Nice suit," I said, sitting down.

The maître d' placed my napkin in my lap. "Your server will be right with you."

"Thank you, Hans," Roy said.

"Seriously," I said again, when Hans had left. "Nice suit."

He smiled, one eyebrow rising just a touch.

"You did this on purpose," I said.

"Couldn't help myself."

"I didn't know you even owned a tie."

"I own a few, actually."

"Why are you making fun of me?"

"Making fun of you? What are you talking about?"

"Did you really have to wear the exact same color I'm wearing?"

"I'm an artist," he said. "Did you ever stop to think this might be my only suit?"

I hedged a moment. Then, "That's bullshit. You're a Wolfe. You could have gone out and bought a suit for tonight if you wanted."

He smiled. "Actually, I own about ten. I hate them all."

"Why the navy blue? Why tonight?"

He sighed. "I don't know. I was feeling feisty, I guess."

"Feisty? I'd say you were feeling like you wanted to mock me. Mock me for wearing professional attire to work. For staying at work late so I could do a good job."

"I admire your work ethic, Charlie. I share it, in fact."

"When it comes to your art."

"Well...yes. My art is my work."

"That's the difference between us, Roy. I appreciate your work. I fully support what you do. You, however, don't afford me the same courtesy."

"That's not true."

"Of course it's true! You hate the clothes I wear to work. You set me up with watercolors and asked me to paint you. Yes, I love art. I might even have a little talent. But it's not my life's work like it is yours."

"Being someone's assistant is your life's work? You're better than that, Charlie."

"Being Lacey's assistant is extremely rewarding."

"Having someone bark orders at you?"

"Have you met Lacey? She doesn't bark orders at anyone. Why are you being such an asshole?"

He didn't reply, just looked down at his menu.

And it struck me. He didn't *know* why he was being an asshole.

But I did.

Something was consuming him. Eating at him. Eating him alive. "What is it, Roy? What did Rock tell you in that meeting? About your sister?"

He didn't reply.

"All right. We don't have to talk about it. But something is bothering you. I'd be an idiot if I couldn't see it."

He twisted his lips, still staring at his menu. "The foie gras is excellent here."

"I don't eat liver."

"This isn't liver. It's foie gras."

"Potato, po-tah-toe."

That got a smile out of him.

He didn't want to tell me? Fine. Two could play this game. I opened my menu. "I think I'll start with the calamari."

"You don't eat liver, but you eat squid?"

"Not squid. *Calamari*." I gave him a saucy smile.

"Mind sharing?"

"What about your foie gras?"

"Reid eats it. I actually hate the stuff."

I couldn't help myself. I burst out in laughter. All right.

Things were calming down now. The server returned and Roy ordered the calamari and a bourbon. Funny, I didn't mind him ordering the calamari for me. Maybe because we were going to share it.

Maybe because he wasn't Blaine Foster.

"Just a glass of water for now," I said, when the server nodded to me.

"Not drinking tonight?" he asked.

"I might have a glass of wine with my dinner. I don't want to overdo it. I have to be in the office early tomorrow."

"Meeting?"

"No. Just a lot of work to do."

Go ahead, I dared him in my mind. Comment about my work again. *I double dare you. I triple dog dare you.*

He kept his mouth shut.

I perused the menu, deciding on an entrée. Trout amandine sounded good. Or the salmon. I wasn't much into red meat.

"Charlie," Roy began.

I looked up and met his gaze. "Yeah?"

"Did you find a therapist for Lacey?"

"Several, actually. I sent her an email before I left. I was able to talk to all of them and explain the situation, and they all felt they could help her."

He cleared his throat. "Would you mind sharing that information?"

"Not at all. With whom?"

Once more, he cleared his throat. "With me."

32

ROY

Guts.

And strength.

I'd used all my guts and strength to ask Charlie for that information. I sat, waiting for her to interrogate me about why I wanted it.

Seconds—that seemed like hours—passed before she said, "Of course I will."

I lifted my brow. Anything else? Wasn't she going to ask why I wanted it? Didn't she care?

"Thanks," I finally said. "Just email me what you emailed to Lacey." I bent back over my menu.

Nothing looked good. My appetite had waned.

Charlie sat across from me like a cross between an innocent angel and a naughty vixen. She was amazing.

She'd understood my painting in the lobby of the Wolfe building.

She might have understood it even better than I did.

She said the painting was hiding something, and she kept looking for a key.

I'd told her there was no key, but was I right?

Why would she be looking if I hadn't left clues for a key?

Maybe a key did exist.

Maybe I just needed some help to find it.

Help from guided hypnosis?

Probably couldn't hurt.

But maybe help from the woman in front of me. The woman who'd helped me reach a new plateau of pleasure. A new plateau of...

The word hovered just above my consciousness, and I captured it.

Love.

I could hardly be in love with a woman I'd only just met.

Though I'd watched my brother fall hard and fast for Lacey.

I wasn't my brother.

Still...I was feeling something, and "love" was the word that had slipped into my consciousness from beyond.

I'd scare her if I confessed that I loved her.

But as I sat, watching her take dainty sips of her water, watching her silver eyes sparkle when the calamari came, watching her wriggle uncomfortably in that damned navy-blue suit...I knew.

I loved her.

I loved Charlie Waters.

Damn.

I'd never allowed those blurred images to surface in my mind. Instead, they lay dormant, their only purpose the mind-fuck I'd lived with for so long.

How long?

How old had I been?

Rock had already left. I'd graduated from high school.

Right.

It was that summer. That last summer before college.

That last summer of what costumed as my youth.

~

THE WOLFE BUILDING.

I hated this place. Had no interest in the family real estate empire. Still, I'd agreed to intern the summer before I left for college. I'd wanted to go straight to art school, but the great Derek Wolfe insisted on a liberal arts degree. Like that would help me ever in my life.

I never actually saw my father, of course. I was the property of one of his many assistants, doing grunt work.

Not that I minded the grunt work. It was easy, and it kept me out of my father's scope. I didn't want to be around him anyway.

Today's grunt task was to move some old records to the lower level.

I loaded the cardboard boxes on the dolly, got into the elevator, and pushed LL, the lowest floor in the building, two floors below the lobby.

The elevator descended, and—

I fell against the wall as the small room dropped rapidly. My stomach lodged in my throat as my flesh prickled. The boxes tumbled off the dolly, banging to the floor.

The red button.

Push the red button.

The lights flickered as I smashed my hand against the crimson disk.

~

"HERE YOU ARE, SIR." The server set a basket of warm bread on the table.

I inhaled, letting the yeasty scent warm me, take away the thoughts that wanted to permeate my brain.

Why? Why would they come now, while I was with the woman I loved?

Yes. Loved.

I couldn't tell her. Couldn't even think about telling her this soon. She'd freak out, and rightly so.

I reached toward the basket, ready to grab a piece of kalamata olive bread, one of my favorites, and then picked up the basket instead and handed it to Charlie.

She smiled, taking it and helping herself to the kalamata bread.

Only one piece, and she took it.

Not that I got stingy with food, but normally I'd be disappointed that I didn't get the bread I wanted.

But I wasn't. If she wanted it, I wanted her to have it.

Must be love.

"You like that olive bread?" I said. "It's my favorite."

"Oh! I'm sorry. Do you want to split it?"

I shook my head. "No. Enjoy it." I reached into the basket and chose a pretzel roll. It was no kalamata olive bread, but a decent substitute.

The server appeared at the side of the table and nodded to Charlie.

"Are you ready to order?"

"Yeah, thank you. I'll start with the house salad with the herb vinaigrette, and then I'll have the trout, please."

"Very good. And you, Mr. Wolfe?"

"House salad, same dressing, and the filet, very rare, with a baked potato."

"Butter or sour cream?"

"Both."

"Excellent. Will you be having wine with dinner?"

"Charlie?" I said.

"Yeah, that would be nice. Something red, but light."

"I have a Beaujolais-Villages that would complement both your meals nicely," he said.

"Great. Bring a bottle." I handed him my menu.

"I'm not sure I can drink more than one glass," Charlie said.

"So?"

"So...you ordered a whole bottle."

"I guess that means I'll drink three glasses, then," I said.

She sighed. "All right, then. You won't be driving me home."

"Charlie, I'm kidding. First, I'd probably be fine to drive after three glasses of wine—"

"And a bourbon," she added.

"And a bourbon. But I probably won't drink three glasses of wine. Who cares?"

"Well, I—" She reddened. "You've never had to watch money in your life, have you?"

"No, but I don't think I'm overly pretentious with my purchases."

"I'm not saying you are."

"You don't have to be a billionaire to leave a little wine in a bottle," he said.

She blushed again. Adorably. "You're right, I suppose."

"Let me treat you to a nice dinner. The only meal we've shared outside my place so far was the one in Helena."

"I don't mean to sound ungrateful."

"You don't sound ungrateful. You sound frugal, but you don't have to be when you're dining with me. It's all on me."

She finally settled down.

Again, I had the desire to talk to her about why I was seeking guided hypnosis.

But should I? Did she deserve to be burdened with that part of me?

I might love her, but I had no idea what her feelings for me were.

"Tell me," I said, "about you and Blaine Foster."

"He's a senior partner at Lacey's old firm."

"I know that much. My father was a client of his. You said you were together. I just want to know the extent of it."

"Just a few months. He wanted to get serious really quickly, and that turned me off. I'm too young, and he's so much older than I am."

Shit.

She didn't want to get serious so quickly.

So much for her possibly returning my feelings.

"Uh-huh," was all I said.

"He's a pretty nice guy, but he did things that annoyed me. Treated me like I was beneath him, you know?"

"How so?"

"For one thing, he always ordered my meal for me, even if I didn't tell him what I wanted yet."

"Then how did he know what you wanted?"

"That's my point. He'd just order something he thought I'd like. Most of the time it was something he liked. Like foie gras."

I laughed at that one. "But you don't eat liver."

"That's what I tried to tell him, but he was convinced I'd love it if I tried it. Even today, when we had lunch, he ordered lasagna for me. I love lasagna, but maybe I wanted something else today, you know?"

"I know."

I knew more than she was aware. My father had constantly tried to change me into something I wasn't. An heir to run the business. Thankfully, Reid had turned out to be interested in running it, and he let me go off to "do my sissy art," as he'd liked to put it.

Do your sissy art.

Get out of here! This has nothing to do with you! Go do your sissy art!

I froze.

33

CHARLIE

Roy's gorgeous face went pale.

I stopped chattering about Blaine and how he liked to control me. At least he hadn't been controlling in the bedroom. Actually, he'd been kind of boring in the bedroom, as if he no longer needed to please a woman because he brought so much else to the table—his position in the community, his money, his power. Not that he was bad in bed— well, his huge cock was great in bed—he just didn't do much. He'd hated going down on me, but of course wanted blow jobs all the time, which were difficult, given his girth. In that regard, he was just like every other man on the planet.

I waited a few seconds, hoping he'd get back to normal.

When he didn't, I said, "Roy?"

He blinked. "Yeah?"

"I think I lost you there for a minute."

"What? No, I'm fine."

He hadn't been fine, but if he wanted to play it that way, I'd go along. Despite our closeness the last few days, I hardly knew the man.

The waiter returned then with our wine. He opened it and poured a tiny portion for Roy to taste. Roy pronounced it fine, so he poured me a glass.

I liked Beaujolais. It was simple. I wanted tonight to be simple. That strange episode Roy had a few minutes ago, though? That had been anything but simple.

After the waiter left again, I regarded him. "What's going on, Roy?"

"Nothing."

"Bull."

"I'm just concerned. About everything. You know. I'm a suspect in my father's murder, for one."

I nodded. I hadn't forgotten. My work so far had all been about that. But this dinner... I sighed. I'd so wanted this dinner to be like the Beaujolais—simple.

But this was Roy Wolfe.

It would never be simple.

"Is there anything you want to talk to me about?"

"My sister."

I nodded. "What about her?"

"I don't think— I don't think she murdered my father."

"I don't think so either, though if what Rock says is true— Lacey filled me in—she sure had a motive."

"I know. But so did we all, if you want to go that route. He didn't sexually abuse Rock, Reid, and me, but he sure abused us physically. And mentally. And emotionally."

Mentally? Emotionally?

Physically, yes. I knew about that, and I ached for Roy and the others for it. Mentally, though? Emotionally?

Roy Wolfe was more complex than I'd imagined.

"I'm so sorry all of you had to go through that."

"We lived," he said, "but I'll be damned if I'm going to spend the rest of my life in prison for something I didn't do. And I don't want my siblings to either."

"Rock has an ironclad alibi."

"The rest of us don't, including Lacey."

I nodded. I didn't know what to say.

"I need help, Charlie."

His voice wasn't weak. It was strong. He was asking for help from a position of strength.

"What can I do?"

"I need to remember, silver. I need to remember."

My skin went cold. "What do you need to remember, Roy?"

"I need to remember what I saw, but God, I don't want to remember."

"What you saw? What are you talking about?"

This was it. This was what I sensed upon our first meeting and what got stronger the more time I spent with Roy Wolfe.

He was hiding something, and now...

Now he wanted the key.

That painting in the lobby when I'd first interacted with Roy. It was so beautiful and haunting. Something was hiding in that painting, and I'd been looking for a key.

Until Roy had said, "There is no key."

"Does this have to do with your father?" I asked.

"Yes, my father. My father and...someone else."

My phone buzzed. Damn! Not now. But it was Lacey, probably about work, and this was still my first week on the job.

"Go ahead and take it," Roy said.

"No. This is more imp—"

"I said take it." His tone wasn't angry, but it was harsh.

I bit my lip. What to do? I answered the call. "Hi, Lace."

"I'm sorry to bother you this late," she said, "but I had a breakthrough, and Rock wants us all to meet back at the office."

"I'm at dinner. With Roy."

"I hate to interrupt your dinner, but this is big. Really big. Roy needs to come too."

"Can't you tell me over the phone?"

Crap. Did I really just say that to my boss who was paying me quadruple what I'd been making before?

"Sorry," I said. "We'll be there."

BACK AT THE office after nine p.m., still dressed in my uncomfortable work clothes. Rock and Lacey were both in jeans, but Reid, of course, still sported his tailored suit. He probably hadn't gone home yet.

"Thanks for coming," Lacey said.

"Thanks for dragging us away from a nice dinner," Roy said sarcastically.

Rock went rigid. "Hey."

"I don't mean any disrespect to any of you," Roy said, "but I'm starving. All I had was some bread and a few calamari."

"We can order in," Lacey suggested. "Rock and I have already eaten."

Roy suppressed an eyeroll. Don't ask me how I knew. I just knew.

Lacey turned to me. "Can you order us some food?"

This time I suppressed an eyeroll. I understood the importance of what was going on, but I had just been at dinner. And now I was supposed to order food for the group? At nine o'clock at night?

Still, I said, "Sure. What do you want?"

"Anything," she said. "Whatever sounds good to the rest of you. I'm not hungry."

"Pizza?" I suggested.

"Works for me," Reid said.

"Me too," from Roy.

I ordered the food quickly.

"Now," Roy said. "You're going to tell Charlie and me why you interrupted our dinner."

34

ROY

Reid regarded me, his eyes wide.

"That's right," I said to him. "Charlie and I were having dinner together."

I purposefully didn't say we were on a "dinner date." I wasn't sure how Charlie would react to that, and I didn't want to rock the boat any more than I already had. I'd let her inside my head a little, and though it was uncomfortable, I felt pretty good about it.

But I didn't want to scare her. Not now. Not when I needed her.

Not when I loved her.

I had to take it slow and easy with Charlie Waters.

Hell, I had to take it slow and easy with myself. I was a fucked up mess, and Charlie deserved a hell of a lot better than a fucked up mess.

Reid didn't reply.

"Anyone have anything to say about that?" I asked.

Four heads, including Charlie's, moved side to side.

"Good. What's up?"

"We were eating dinner, and Lace remembered something on that signature page."

"Yeah," Lacey said. "There were three signatures. One was Derek's, I assume, and the other was the woman Blaine mentioned, the one with an unusual name. Then there was a third."

"A third?" Reid asked.

"Yeah. The agreement was between three people. I can't remember the woman's name. Not yet, anyway. But I'm pretty sure the other man's name was James."

"First or last?" Reid asked.

"First. I can't recall the last name. I just remember thinking at the time that it was the same name as James Earl Jones. I'd just watched a documentary that he narrated, so he was in my head. You know, his voice kind of permeates you."

"You don't think it was James Jones, though?"

"No. That I definitely would have remembered. It just came to me while Rock and I were eating, and we had a documentary on TV."

"Narrated by James Earl Jones?"

"No, someone with an English accent, actually. But you know how things just remind you of something and then pop into your mind, right? That's what happened. I'd watched a documentary, I can't even remember what it was about, the night before, and James Earl Jones's voice was in my head, and I saw the name James on the page."

"James," Reid said. "James. Who did Dad know named James?"

"Probably about a million people," Rock said. "But at least it's a start."

"Someone with whom he'd be entering into some kind of confidential settlement under the table," Reid said. "That might narrow it down a little. I know most of his business contacts."

"Any named James?" Lacey asked.

"Several that I can think of offhand, and I'm sure there are more. I guess I start making calls."

"James," Charlie said softly. "I always liked that name. It sounds so strong and regal."

I smiled. She was sweet.

"Of course," she went on, "we have the most regal name of all right here in this room. You know that Roy means king, don't you?"

I nodded. "In French. Yeah."

Rock and Reid both stared at me.

"What?" I finally said.

Rock cleared his throat. "Okay, so Reid's going to search for contacts named James. You might want to add Jim, too."

Jim.

I jerked my head.

Jim.

Father Jim.

And I knew who we were looking for.

35

CHARLIE

R oy went white.

I stopped myself from showing my surprise.

No one else seemed to notice. Was it possible I already knew this man better than his own brothers did?

I itched to touch him, to soothe him, offer him comfort. Comfort for what?

Why had he tensed up? Gone pale?

Rock and Reid kept talking, Lacey adding bits and pieces as well, but I'd stopped listening. I focused on Roy, his needs, though I had no idea what those needs actually were.

My phone buzzed, and I nearly jumped out of my seat.

"Everything okay?" Lacey asked.

"Yeah, fine. It's just...the pizza's here. I'll go down and get it."

Roy stood then. "I'll go with you."

I nodded, and the two of us left the conference room.

When we stepped into the elevator, I flashed back to the first time Roy and I had gone downstairs to pick up food. Only days had passed, but it almost felt like a lifetime. So much had happened since then.

He didn't talk. We just descended—

Right as we hit the first floor, he fell against the wall, grasping at the small railing inside the elevator.

"Roy! Are you okay?"

He nodded. "I was just thinking about..."

"About what?"

"About one time. In an elevator."

I'd been in an elevator with him several times. Never had I seen a reaction like this one.

"You okay?" I asked. "You want to wait here, and I'll get the pizza?"

He shook his head. "I'm okay."

We walked together through the lobby and to the locked doorway. We grabbed the pizzas from the delivery guy and then locked back up.

"Still warm," I said. "Good. I'm starving."

"I'm sorry about our dinner," Roy said.

"Why? It wasn't your fault, and this is important. We need all the information we can get to figure out who's responsible for your father's murder."

He nodded and then walked away from me...and toward the painting that had caught my eye my first morning here.

I followed him, standing a few feet behind him. "It's so beautiful," I said.

"The key," he said softly.

"What?"

He turned to me, his dark eyes taking on an almost wild look.

"The key," he said again. "I think I may have found it."

"The key?" I wrinkled my brow. "Oh, right."

I stared at the painting. The first time I'd seen it, I'd told him I sensed something hidden, and I was looking for a key. "You said there isn't one."

"But there is now," he said, his voice taking on a faraway sound.

"Where? Where is the key, Roy?"

He pointed to his head. "In here."

He said nothing more as he walked to the elevator. I followed him in silence. We ascended in silence.

When we returned to the conference room, I handed out the pizza on paper plates.

Roy didn't speak for the rest of the meeting.

I ENDED up at my own place that evening.

Roy hadn't invited me to his place, and I hadn't invited him to mine. I sensed that he needed to be alone. Could I have been wrong? Possibly, but not likely.

My tummy was sticking out from overindulgence in the pizza. It was so late, and I'd been so hungry that I'd gorged on four pieces. Now I had a night of indigestion ahead of me.

I rooted around for the Pepto-Bismol, Roy's painting never leaving my mind.

The key.

The key was in his head.

I was right. Roy was hiding something. Maybe he hadn't realized he was hiding it. Now he knew.

Something had occurred to him while we were on the elevator —something that had made him react by clamping onto the wall.

Then the painting.

The key.

He wasn't ready to talk about the key yet. That was obvious. But he had asked me to share with him the names of the therapists I'd found who practiced guided hypnosis.

He was ready to pursue something.

Maybe.

I had to go to work tomorrow. Would Roy be there? He didn't always come into the office.

So I'd go to him. I set my alarm for an hour earlier.

Tomorrow morning, I was going to Roy's.

I was going to help him find the key.

36

ROY

Elevator.

The elevator.

How had I forgotten so much?

How?

Easy. I'd forgotten because I'd had to live with what I'd seen. What I'd encountered. What I could never *un*see.

Not unless I shoved it into a locked chest in the farthest part of my mind.

I'd done it.

All this time, I knew it was there, but I never allowed myself to see it. So many years had passed that I almost convinced myself it was my imagination. Just a horrible image that I'd once created.

After all, I was an artist.

A creator.

Creations weren't always beautiful. Sometimes they were vicious. Sometimes they were ugly.

Sometimes they were from the depths of hell.

The elevator.

The goddamned elevator.

James.

James Earl Jones.

Reid's contacts named James.

Named Jim.

Jim.

Father Jim.

Why did I abhor Father Jim? Father Jim wasn't one of those pedophilic priests the church protected. Father Jim had never touched me or my brothers. Or my sister, as far as I knew.

He'd baptized all of us, given us our first communion.

In return, Derek Wolfe had kept his parish alive with massive donations.

Donations to a church, to the nearby convent, to their food pantry and their shelters.

Derek Wolfe, who hadn't given two shits about the hungry and the homeless.

Why?

Why?

Why?

The key.

The key.

I had the key now.

All I had to do was insert it into the lock, turn it, and...

Find the truth.

The truth I'd been hiding.

The truth that had fucked with my mind for so damned long.

Was I ready?

Even if I was ready, would it help the current situation?

It might.

It might not.

But one thing was certain.

It could help me.

I could finally be free of what plagued me. What was always there, in the back of my brain, fucking with me.

Fear cloaked me.

What if I needed it? Needed it for my art? What if I was only able to create because of my struggle?

I couldn't give up my art.

Couldn't.

So only one thing to do.

Bury the key.

37

CHARLIE

I inhaled deeply, adjusting my dark red skirt. I'd splurged on several new suits when Lacey had offered me the new position, but I'd been a little wary of wearing the red.

Today, though, I wanted to knock Roy's socks off so he'd talk to me. It was early, and he might still be in bed, but I rang for him anyway.

"Yeah?" came his voice from the intercom.

I cleared my throat. "It's me. I mean...it's Charlie."

Nothing for a moment. Then, "Come on up." The door buzzed open.

I kept myself from hyperventilating in the elevator.

The elevator.

Although not this building, the elevator was where Roy had freaked out last night. What was it about an elevator?

I'd come here for one reason—to help Roy find the key. Whatever the key was. The key, I was sure, was some kind of metaphor. We weren't looking for a real key, of course. But what was the key a metaphor for?

Roy was ready to open up. He'd asked me for the names of the therapists who could do guided hypnosis.

I sighed. It wasn't my place to try to get information out of him, but here I was anyway, clad in daring red—

The elevator door opened. I walked slowly toward Roy's door.

As I lifted my hand to knock, Roy opened the door.

I sucked in a breath. He was wearing nothing but a pair of white lounging pants. His abs smacked me upside the head. He was so magnificent. His hair was a mass of disarray hanging around his shoulders. Smears of paint—blues, mostly—striped his chest, arms, and hands.

"I-I'm sorry," I stammered. "I woke you up."

He shook his head. "I didn't sleep."

"You were painting."

He nodded.

Odd, that he hadn't pulled his hair from his eyes.

"What are you working on?"

"Something new."

"May I—"

"No. It's not ready yet."

"Have you—"

"No," he said again. "I haven't looked at your watercolor."

"But you had to move it, to get ready to paint, right?"

"I'm capable of moving a painting that's covered off the easel without looking at it, Charlie."

Charlie again. Not silver.

Roy was...not Roy.

Or maybe he *was* Roy. Maybe I really didn't know Roy at all, despite the closeness we'd shared. After all, only days had passed...

"I didn't mean to suggest—"

"I told you I wouldn't look at it, and I never break my word."

His dark eyes seared into me. "I know. I mean, I didn't—"

His lips came down on mine.

Hard.

Raw.

Almost intimidating.

Yet full of need. Full of yearning need.

I had to leave in an hour to get to work on time. I was dressed in a brand new suit. I couldn't ruin it with blue oil paint. Couldn't...

My mind went blank as I returned his kiss, the fresh scent of hand soap edging into his natural woodsy aroma of musk.

I inhaled through my nose, drinking in the fragrance of his torment, of his secrets.

Of his key.

Of him.

This was all part of Roy Wolfe.

And Roy Wolfe was...

God, no. I wasn't Lacey. I wasn't going to fall in love in a week. Not when...

Not when...

His tongue searched my mouth, twirling with mine, our lips sliding together. When I finally needed to take a deep breath, I pulled away, and he caught my lower lip between his teeth and bit. Not hard.

But not softly either.

Just right. Just fucking right.

I inhaled when he finally let my lip drop.

"Bedroom," he said huskily.

Bedroom.

Leave for work in an hour.

All doable.

He took my arm—more gently than I expected—and led me to his bedroom.

Sure enough, the bed was made. He hadn't slept, as he'd said.

Which meant he was tired.

He wasn't acting tired. He was acting...

Again, all thoughts melded together into only desire. Only passion. Only need for Roy's body inside mine.

"Suit," he said huskily. "At least it's a good color this time. But it's not you, silver. It's not you."

Yeah, he didn't like my clothes. We'd been through that. He didn't—

He yanked my blazer off my shoulders, and it fell to the floor in a blood-red heap. I looked down at the front of my white blouse.

Blues and grays streaked the pale silk. I dropped my mouth open.

"Who cares?" he said, as if reading my thoughts.

"I do. I have to go to work."

"We'll get you a new blouse." He looked down at the jacket. "And blazer."

"I paid a lot for this suit."

"I'll have it cleaned for you."

"That's not the point. I have to—"

Lips on mine again. If possible, he kissed me even harder this time, ravaging my mouth like a wild beast feasting on its prey.

I resisted at first, only because of work and my clothes, and then—

Just the kiss once more. Just Roy. Just me. Just this kiss.

Just us.

Nothing else mattered.

Work?

No.

My soiled clothing?

No.

Nothing.

Only us. Only now.

I quickly unbuttoned my blouse, our mouths fused together, only because if I didn't I was afraid he'd rip it off me. I shimmied out of my skirt for the same reason.

There.

All good. Only my pumps, bra, and panties separated me from being naked and in Roy's arms.

He broke the kiss and inhaled deeply. His cock was hard and tented his lounge pants. I couldn't resist. I dropped to my knees and freed it.

Bigger and more beautiful than ever, it sprang majestically from its ebony nest, a clear pearl of liquid at its tip. I licked it off, letting the saltiness tingle on my tongue before I swallowed.

No. Shouldn't suck him. Should fuck him and get it over with. Get to work. Get to work.

I ignored my conscience and flicked my tongue over his head. He shuddered, a soft moan creeping from his throat. He was so responsive, and that turned me on even more. I took him inside my mouth, held him there for a moment, letting his knob touch the back of my throat, and then I reversed the movement, slowly sliding my lips off him.

All the way off him.

Then I began again.

I didn't have time for this. Didn't have time to torment him until he was ready to explode.

Didn't have—

I took him deep within my mouth again, letting my tongue swirl over his length.

Slowly I sucked him, each time getting more used to the invasion at the back of my throat. Each time wanting more and more to please him.

Each time forgetting more and more what was at stake.

I expected him to grab my hair as he had before, force me to go faster, to take more of him.

But he didn't. He seemed content for me to take the lead, to suck long and slow, to—

He pulled out of my mouth. "I need to fuck you."

His words were raw, his voice deep and husky, his demeanor animalistic.

And I was so, so ready.

He was even more ready. He ripped my panties off me—yes, literally ripped them in two—lifted me in his arms, and set me down on his hard cock.

The burn. The burn of being sliced into so quickly and unexpectedly.

God, it was good.

Roy gripped my hips and moved me up and down on his cock, still standing by his bed. Not against the wall. Not leaning on anything. Just his pure raw strength holding us both upright.

My tits were still encased in my bra, but they bounced anyway, abrading his chest as he fucked me, fucked me, fucked me.

Faster. Faster. Faster. Fast—

"Ah!" He brought me down so hard as he released, that I felt as if he were reaching far into my body, farther than anyone ever had, far into my soul. The depths of my soul.

"Fuck, silver," he grunted. "Fuck. I love you."

38

ROY

I *love you.*
I love you.
Fuck. I love you.

The climax swept through me like a herd of raging bulls. They trampled over the vast grass, their hooves bringing up clouds of dusty earth. All inside me, they raged, as I took from this woman's body what I needed. What I craved.

I love you.

Fuck. I love you.

Then a voice. A sweet melodic voice. The voice of my angel.

"You... You love me?"

Reality hit me in the head like a boulder tumbling from a mountain.

You love me?

God, yes. I loved her. But had I said it? Out loud?

Fuck! It was too soon. She'd go running. She'd go running far away from me.

My cock slid out of her and I placed her gently on my bed. What to say? What *could* I say?

It was the truth. I loved her.

She looked up at me, her eyes innocent and questioning.

And I melted.

"Yeah, silver. Yeah. I love you. I really love you."

I hoped for a smile.

I didn't get one.

She bit on her lower lip as it trembled. Finally, she spoke. "I didn't come."

"I know. I'm sorry."

"No. That's not what I mean. I mean... Oh, shit. I don't know what I mean."

"You don't have to say it back." *Except that you do. Please say it back.*

"I..."

I sat down next to her. "You don't have—"

She reached forward and pressed two fingers against my lips. "I know. I actually...want to say it back. But it's only been..."

I kissed her lips softly. "I know."

"Are you sure?" she asked timidly.

"Silver, I've never been more sure of anything. I can promise you that."

No truer words. I was unsure of pretty much everything in my brain...except for the fact that I loved this beautiful woman.

"I..."

"Silver."

"I want to say it back. I wasn't lying."

"I know. If you want to say it back, that means you're feeling it, right?"

She nodded shyly.

"Then I can wait. You say it when you're ready."

Funny thing was, I wasn't ready myself. It had come out on its own. I'd only been thinking the words, or so I'd thought.

She looked down at her blouse. "What am I going to wear to work?"

"We'll go shopping."

"At seven-thirty in the morning?"

"Right. Well...you can wear one of my shirts."

"Your shirts will hang on me."

Yeah, she was right. "Your skirt is okay. A little wrinkled, but okay. You just need..." I stood and walked over to my closet. I didn't have a vast wardrobe like Reid did. My clothing consisted mostly of jeans, shirts, T-shirts, and paint smocks. A few pairs of shorts. And of course those ten damned suits that I hated wearing.

I looked through my shirts, and—

"Here." I held up a red women's shirt. "This will work."

"The reds aren't quite— Wait a minute. Whose *is* that?"

Whose indeed? I clawed at my memory. I'd had little contact with women. Only a few—

"Just someone I hooked up with once. She left it here. It was a year ago, at least."

She didn't look convinced.

"Silver, there's been no one since you."

"It's only been a week."

"Which means I couldn't possibly be lying to you. You've been with me nearly nonstop." I tossed her the shirt. "This is it. Either that or you call in."

She threw the shirt back at me. "I'll go home and change."

"You might be late for work."

She bit her lip again. God, she looked adorable. Would Charlie chance being late for a brand new job?

She stood impudently and picked up the shirt. "It'll do." She grabbed her skirt and marched into the bathroom.

And I tried not to chuckle out loud.

She'd be going to work commando today.

And I wouldn't be able to stop thinking about that.

She came out of the bathroom, her hair freshly brushed, the

skirt looking nearly wrinkle free. The stretchy V-neck shirt was tight on her, which made her breasts look amazing, and she was right. The reds didn't quite match, but only she and I would notice that. We had painters' eyes. They were close enough.

"Close enough," she agreed, when I mentioned it. Then, instead of hurrying out as I expected her to, she sat back down on the bed.

"Don't you need—"

"In fifteen minutes. I can make it if I leave in fifteen minutes."

Worked for me. I began lowering my pajama pants.

She held up her hand. "No, that's not what I meant. I didn't come here to...have sex. I really didn't."

"We just had sex, silver."

"Yeah. I was there. But I came to talk to you."

"Oh?" I sat down next to her. "What about?"

"About the key."

My skin chilled, so much that I rubbed my upper arms to ease the cold.

The key.

The key I needed to bury for my sanity.

The key I needed to unearth to save my family.

The key only Charlie knew about.

"I told you the first time in the lobby. There is no key."

She touched my cheek, the palm of her hand so warm against my now freezing skin. "There's a key. You already admitted it to me earlier. You're hiding it, Roy. And it's killing you."

39

CHARLIE

He didn't deny my words.

I hadn't meant to be so blunt. Whatever was inside him wasn't literally killing him, but it was eating him up. Something about what Lacey had recalled had him spooked.

"It's the name," I said. "James."

"James," he said softly. "Jim."

"Right. Jim. Who is it, Roy? Who is Jim?"

He didn't answer, not that I expected him to. I glanced at my watch. I had twelve minutes now. Twelve minutes to uncover something that was probably buried under layers and layers of memories in Roy's subconscious.

"He's a priest," Roy said finally. "Father Jim is a priest."

I wasn't Catholic, but I knew well the stories of priests who had behaved very badly. The thought of—

"He didn't do anything to me. To any of us."

"Not to you. Not to the Wolfes. That's what you're saying."

He nodded. "Not to kids."

I let out a breath I hadn't realized I'd been holding. "Thank God."

"But he..." Roy closed his eyes. "The elevator."

"Were you in an elevator with Father Jim?"

"No. I was eighteen, I think. Nineteen maybe. The summer before college."

"And he...?" I swallowed. *Please don't let this go there. Not Roy. Not my Roy.*

"He was in the building. With my father. The Wolfe building."

"Where I work?"

He cleared his throat. "Yeah. Only I wasn't supposed to see..."

"See what, Roy? What weren't you supposed to see?"

He closed his eyes. "Don't. Don't make me do this." His body trembled.

I touched his face again. It was icy beneath my fingertips.

"Hey," I said, my heart racing. "Easy. Open your eyes. Look at me."

He obeyed, his dark eyes searing into my own.

"It's okay. You don't have to do this. Not right now."

"I can't," he said.

"I know. I understand."

"No, you don't understand." He sighed. "I can't do it right now. I can't do it...ever."

My sweet, sweet Roy. His eyes were more troubled than I'd ever seen them.

"Just tell me for sure that nothing happened to you. Please. I have to know you're okay."

"Nothing happened to me, silver," he said. "But I'm far from okay."

Five minutes. Stupid fucking watch! I had five minutes before I had to leave to get to work on time. How could I leave him? How could I leave this man I loved when he was so distraught?

"Go," he said. "Get to work. I know it's important to you."

"You're important to me too."

"I've lived this long without the key. I can live another hundred years if I have to. Go. Please."

I scraped my fingers over his dark stubble. "Roy..."

"Do I have to force you to leave?"

I stood. I had to. The job. Lacey. The commitment. Everything.

Roy.

Everything.

Roy was a part of everything.

"I'll go," I said, "but this isn't over. I'm coming straight over here after work tonight, and we're going to finish this conversation."

Roy said nothing. Just sat, as if numb, while I let myself out.

THANK GOD FOR BUSYWORK. I got to hide in my office for most of the day making phone calls. Worked for me, since my breasts were on full display in another woman's stretchy shirt.

At least we didn't have a meeting in the conference room today, which meant I wouldn't see Roy. I needed to keep thoughts of him at bay so I could get my work done. I worked on the memorial service with Terrence, and then I set up what seemed like a million—but was only eleven—appointments for Lacey.

Back to the memorial service.

Next on my list.

Call priest at St. Andrew's Parish and reconfirm time at the church.

Easy enough. I found the number and placed the call.

"St. Andrew's."

"Hi there. This is Charlie Waters at Wolfe Enterprises. I need to speak to..." What was his name? I had no idea. "The parish priest to confirm our memorial service for Mr. Wolfe."

"Oh, of course. Let me connect you."

A few seconds passed. Then,

"Father Jim here."

My stomach dropped and my skin went cold.

Father Jim. Was this Roy's Father Jim?

I cleared my throat. "Yes, hello, Father. This is Charlie Waters at Wolfe Enterprises. I'm just calling to reconfirm the memorial service for next week." Another throat clear. "For Mr. Wolfe. Er... Derek Wolfe."

"Yes, of course. It's all scheduled on our end."

"All right. Thank you, Father."

"Not a problem. Happy to do it. Mr. Wolfe was a huge supporter of our parish. Did you know I gave all the Wolfe children their first communion?"

"No, I didn't. That's...interesting."

"Tell me. Have you heard from Riley?"

"We haven't. We've got the best PIs looking for her. I'm sure she won't want to miss her father's service."

The lie tasted like moldy vegetables in my mouth. Why would Riley want to go to a memorial service for the man who molested her for her entire life?

"I'm not sure that's the case, Ms. Waters," Father Jim said through the phone. "Derek did dote on Riley, but her brothers have probably poisoned her against him."

What? I wasn't sure what to say about that, so I changed the subject. "Thank you for your time, Father. I look forward to your service."

"We'll do it up Wolfe style, just the way Derek would have wanted," he said.

Wolfe style? This was a memorial service, not a gala event.

Though from what I'd seen of the wake plans at the Waldorf, it might as well be a gala. The portion at the church, though? That should be sacred and solemn.

"I'm sure everything will be perfect," I said. "Thank you, Father. Goodbye."

"Ms. Waters?"

"Yes?"

"How are the boys doing?"

"The boys?"

"Derek's sons, of course. I hear Rock is home and is heading up the company."

"That's what Mr. Wolfe's will mandated. Yes."

"And Reid? How is he taking it?"

I cleared my throat. "I'm not sure I should be talking about my bosses."

"Oh, don't be silly. I've known all of them since they were little. They're like my own kids, in a way. I'm sure Reid was disappointed that Derek didn't choose him to take over the business."

Hmm. Maybe Father Jim had some insight into Derek Wolfe.

"Father, may I ask you a question?"

"Of course, dear."

"Why would Derek Wolfe have forced Rock to come back to New York? If you know, that is. Everyone was surprised by it."

"I've known Derek Wolfe for decades," he said, "and nothing he ever did surprised me, including this."

"I'm not sure what that means."

"It means, dear, that Derek Wolfe calculated everything he did in life. Everything had to lead to some kind of gain."

"Financial, you mean."

"My dear, financial gains aren't the only type of gains in the world."

"But Derek Wolfe was a businessman. He built an empire. To turn it over to a person unprepared to take the lead seems so..."

"Strange? Odd?" he said.

"Well...yeah."

"But not surprising. At least not to me. He did it for some kind of gain."

"Why? He's dead. He no longer has anything to gain."

"Not financially, no."

"Not in any way, Father. The man is dead."

"He is, yes."

None of this was making any kind of sense. "All right, Father. Thank you for your time."

"You're most welcome, Ms. Waters. And if I may add one more piece of advice?"

"Uh...sure." I guess.

"Derek Wolfe was a master manipulator. His success came at a cost, as everything does. But he never took his eyes off the gain, whatever gain he was after."

"That's hardly a piece of advice. Why are you telling me this?"

"Just being a good Samaritan, dear. Goodbye."

I sat for a moment, staring at the wall in my office. I really should get a piece of artwork to hang there. For now, it was a blank wall. A blank screen.

A blank screen.

A blank...

A thought probed into my head.

I had to see Roy.

40

ROY

Charlie hadn't been kidding. She showed up at my place right after work. I'd already ordered food. I hadn't thought for a minute that she wouldn't show.

I'd had the day to figure out my plan. How to get her off this key business.

How to get myself off this key business.

I hadn't come up with anything.

I'd painted all day, working on the piece I'd started yesterday. It was an abstract in blues and grays.

I stood, staring at her as she walked in after I opened the door, looking completely at home in my place. I liked that. I liked that a lot.

And damn, that red shirt looked way hotter on her than it had on whatever her name was.

I expected her to want to get right down to business—she'd expect me to start spilling about the key or lack thereof.

But she didn't.

She gave me a quick hug and then pressed something into my hand.

I looked down. It was a business card.

"Dr. Alison Woolcott?" I asked.

"Yup. The best in the state, I've heard."

"At what?"

She cleared her throat. "Guided hypnosis. I made an appointment for Lacey today."

"Oh."

"That's who Lace chose, but if you're more comfortable with a male therapist, she has a partner, Dr. Brett Aldrich, who's supposed to be nearly as good."

"I...uh..."

"No pressure," she said. "You go on your own time. But..."

"But what?"

"Your own time is of the essence, with all of you being persons of interest in your dad's murder."

I couldn't help a chuckle. "Go on my own time, you say. But not on my own time, really."

She sighed. "Roy, it's up to you. But it's also up to you to get to the bottom of this if you think it will help you and your brothers and sister. You know that. You don't need me to spell it out for you."

I nodded. What else could I do?

"When is Lacey going in?"

"Monday at noon. Over lunch. It was all Dr. Woolcott had available on such short notice, other than evenings."

"She was willing to give up her lunch hour?"

"Lace? Or the doctor? They both were."

"Why?"

"Lace because she wants to remember the name of the woman on the settlement agreement. The doctor because we're paying three times her normal fee."

"I see. That doesn't bode well for a doctor."

"It bodes just fine. We offered."

"She didn't have to accept."

"Why wouldn't she? If someone asked me to skip lunch to do my normal work for three times what I make in an hour, I'd do it like that." She snapped her fingers.

She was right. I was just being a pain for the sake of being a pain. And the fact that guided hypnosis scared the shit out of me.

"If she's booked—"

"She has evening hours. It costs a little more, but I think you might be able to afford it."

"Ha ha," I said. "I ordered dinner."

She inhaled. "I can tell. It smells great. Italian?"

"Northern Italian, yeah."

"We'll have to eat quickly, then. Your appointment is at eight."

I twisted my head so far I nearly cracked my neck. "Say what?"

"I took the liberty of—"

"So all that 'in your own time' was bullshit, huh?"

"No."

"Give me a break."

"It wasn't bullshit, Roy. I told Dr. Woolcott you might not be up for it, and if that was the case, I'd call her by seven. You have a little less than half an hour to decide."

I shook my head. "Oh my God. You had no right—"

"Stop right there. I had every right. I'm the woman you love, remember?"

"The woman I love who can't say it back."

"I love you, okay? I love you. I love you, I love you, I love you."

God she was beautiful. Like a platinum rose in the wind— that feisty wind right before a thunderstorm.

Yet I had no doubt of her sincerity.

She loved me.

The fiery silver in her eyes showed me that love more than words ever could.

"So...?" she prodded.

I didn't reply.

"I was staring at the blank wall in my office today, thinking it was like a blank screen that I could cover with art, and a thought popped into my head. Your mind is blank right now. You won't let the key do its work. This therapist can help you, can put art back onto your wall."

I gazed at her, at the excitement in her gorgeous eyes.

"Don't tell me you haven't had the same thought. You're the one who asked me to give you the therapists' names in the first place."

"Let's eat," I said simply.

"Have it your way." She looked at her watch. "You still have twenty-four minutes to decide."

Charlie pulled out paper plates and utensils and dished out the takeout. She looked comfortable in my tiny kitchen, like she belonged there.

She *did* belong there.

I wanted her here. I wanted her here for good.

Damn. A week! We'd known each other for little more than a week. But we'd traveled together in that time, we'd painted each other—I still hadn't looked at her portrait—and we'd made amazing passionate love.

"I love you," I said.

She smiled, handing me a plate of chicken and pasta. "I know. I love you too."

I looked down at the food. One of my favorite restaurants, but I had no appetite. Finally I met Charlie's gaze. Her sweet lips glistened.

"Charlie," I said, "what should I do?"

"Only you can answer that question, Roy."

Nope. She wasn't going to let me cop out. Not that I thought she might. I knew, as soon as I asked, what her response would be.

How was she so strong? So sure of herself?

She'd had a modest life. A life of poverty compared to mine. Yet she came out unscathed. Surely she had her baggage. Everyone did. But still...

What would Charlie do?

Indeed, that was the question, and I already knew the answer.

"I'll go," I said.

She smiled, so beautiful. "I knew you would."

"But it might not help at all."

"True. It might not. And it will probably take several sessions before anything happens. But it's a step, Roy. A crucial first step. And I'm happy for you."

41

CHARLIE

Roy began eating then, and soon his plate was empty. He laughed. "I didn't think I was hungry."

"You weren't, until you made the decision to help yourself. This is a good thing." I took a sip of the red wine I'd poured for us. "What did you do today?"

"I worked on a new piece, the one I began yesterday."

"I thought maybe you'd take a nap."

He scoffed lightly. "I tried, but I couldn't."

"I have a feeling you'll sleep like a baby tonight."

"Maybe. I will if you're next to me."

"I suppose that can be arranged. Tomorrow is Saturday so I don't have to worry about getting to work. I don't have any clothes here, though."

"So? I'm thinking you won't need a lot of clothes for what I want to do."

My cheeks warmed. This was still so new. So new and wonderful.

The beginning part of relationships was always so exciting. Talking and making love and talking and making love.

And going out of town on a private jet.

And going with your new boyfriend to see a guided hypnotist.

Yeah. Normal stuff.

Well, the Wolfes were hardly normal. They were billionaires who owned a major real estate corporation and a private jet. A jet I'd flown in, no less.

I looked at my watch quickly. "You want any more? We have about five minutes."

"No. I'm good."

"Great. Now go change your clothes quickly. I'll get us a cab."

"We need to leave now?"

"I guess we have about twenty minutes."

His gaze melted me. "I know exactly what we can do."

Seconds later I was bent over the couch, Roy ramming his hard cock into me. It was raw, it was feral, and it was spectacular.

"I love you," he said through gritted teeth. "I fucking love you, silver."

"I love you too, Roy," I nearly wept, my body trembling as he thrust into me again and again. The couch was leather with a crocheted afghan over the back. The wool of the afghan tickled my clit as he pumped, and soon I was soaring into a fiery climax.

I balled my hands into fists, moaned and screamed, as my body sank farther into the couch as he plunged, plunged, plunged.

The orgasm roared through me, my pussy throbbing in time with my heart, until finally Roy pushed into me deeply, violently, and released. Every pulse of his cock, every beat of his heart, every ounce of love from his soul wrapped me in ecstasy.

And I knew.

I fucking knew.

This was my forever.

∼

"NERVOUS?" I patted Roy's thigh in the back of the cab.

"No." He looked straight ahead.

"Liar." I smiled. "It's okay to be nervous."

"I know. I'm not all Alpha like Rock and Reid."

"Oh, you're pretty Alpha, from what I've seen." I squeezed his hard thigh.

"They're both so...strong."

"So are you, Roy. So are you."

He nodded. "In some ways."

"Don't sell yourself short. This is for your family, for sure. But this is ultimately for you. To free you of whatever is inside you, whatever you're hiding."

"It's been there for so long," he said. "Most of the time I forget about it."

He wasn't lying. But he was. He thought he forgot about it, but he never did. I'd sensed that the first time I talked to him in the lobby about his painting.

Had he titled that painting? I'd never asked. I wasn't sure now was the time to ask.

"You said you were working on a new project," I said. "I didn't get a chance to go into your studio and take a look. Tell me about it."

He yawned. "It's...personal."

He hadn't slept last night. He was obviously fatigued. Maybe this eight o'clock therapy appointment wasn't such a great idea after all.

But he'd agreed. I wasn't about to turn back the clock now.

The cab stopped at the large building in downtown Manhattan. We were only a block away from the Wolfe Building.

Roy paid the cabbie. The building loomed tall and dark in front of us. The sun hadn't set quite yet but was behind a cloud, and the grayish exterior seemed almost ghostly.

But it was a building. Only a building. I entwined my fingers with Roy's and squeezed his hand.

He nodded. He got the message. *Everything is all right.* That's what my squeeze meant. I hoped my squeeze wasn't lying.

We entered the building. Because it was after hours, we had to sign in with the lobby attendant, and he entered a code for us to go up in the elevator.

Roy tensed visibly.

Something about elevators.

Odd, since he'd been using elevators his whole life. Only now had I noticed how much they bothered him.

Maybe I should try to break the ice. "Ever had sex in an elevator?" I asked, trying to sound light and airy.

He cleared his throat, didn't smile. "Never had the urge."

Funny. That first day, when we came down in the elevator to get the lunch for our conference meeting, I bet he'd have been singing a different tune.

"You've never been in an elevator with me before," I said playfully. Of course, he *had* been in an elevator with me before, several times.

"Silver, I'll gladly fuck you as many times as you want. Just not right now, and not in an elevator."

Hmm. Weird. Roy didn't like elevators? How had I never noticed that?

I squeezed his hand once more as the elevator dinged and stopped at our floor.

We followed the signage to the offices of Drs. Woolcott and Aldrich. Roy stopped in front of the door. I inhaled, grasped the knob, and entered.

To my surprise, a young woman sat at the reception desk. Since it was after hours, I'd assumed we'd be entering an empty office.

"Hi," she said brightly. "Are you Dr. Woolcott's eight o'clock?"

Roy nodded. "I am."

"I'll let her know you're here. Have a seat." She gestured to me. "We have lots of magazines for you to look at while you're waiting."

I nodded. Yeah. Right. Just what I needed. Leaf through *Cosmo* while the man I loved was inside spilling his guts to a stranger.

My nerves were on edge. Really on edge.

And I wasn't even the one getting hypnotized.

An older woman, pretty with some gray at her temples, stepped out from behind an oak door. She walked toward us. "Mr. Wolfe?"

Roy stood.

"I'm Alison Woolcott." She held out her hand. "It's a pleasure."

"Thanks for staying open late for me."

"Not at all. We don't all keep to normal schedules, and I'm here for whoever needs me." She turned to me, her hand still out. "Alison Woolcott."

"Charlie Waters," I said. "I'm just here for moral support."

"That's kind of you. I'll try not to keep him too long. But this is my last appointment today, so if we start getting somewhere, do you want to keep going?"

"Yeah," Roy said. "Let's get it over with."

Dr. Woolcott smiled. "I understand your trepidation. But I should warn you. Things are rarely resolved in one session."

Roy nodded and then looked to me. "You don't have to stay."

"Of course I do. If you need me, I'll be right out here."

"Ready?" Dr. Woolcott gestured to her office door.

Roy nodded tentatively. I smiled, trying to give him strength. Inside, though, my stomach was in knots.

Really *knotted* knots.

It'll be okay, I said silently.

Whether I was talking to Roy or to myself, I wasn't sure.

42

ROY

The office was decorated sparsely, which surprised me. "You need to focus," the doc was saying. "I don't want anything in this room to detract from what we're doing." Had I asked about the sparse décor? I didn't think I had.

Must be part of her standard spiel.

"Most patients are more comfortable in the recliner." She motioned to a dark-brown leather chair. "But I also have the couch. Or just a regular chair if you prefer."

"I guess I'll try the recliner." I walked to it and sat down.

She took a seat opposite me in her leather desk chair. "We'll deal with paperwork later. I'll email it to you, and you can send it back the same way. I don't want to waste time with red tape when we can be getting down to business."

"Is that how you always work?"

She shook her head. "Usually I email the paperwork in advance, but this appointment was only made today."

"Right." I looked around, twisting my head to look behind me. Her credentials were on the wall behind me, clearly part of her focusing plan. The patient couldn't stare at the doctor's myriad degrees on the wall. Dr. Woolcott had an M.D. from the University of Vermont. Not Harvard, but not bad. She also had several certifications in hypnotic therapy. Good. Good.

"I assure you I'm highly qualified."

"Oh, I didn't mean—"

"It's okay. Every new patient does it. My partner and I have had countless other professionals accuse us of practicing voodoo, but hypnosis is real, and it's very effective."

I said nothing.

"Have you been having any symptoms?"

"Like what? I'm in perfect health."

"Stress, Mr. Wolfe. Nervousness? Rapid heartbeat?"

"No. Not really."

She scribbled some notes on her pad.

"What can I help you with today?"

"I need to find something."

"Something you lost?"

"In a way. There's something in the back of my mind. Something I don't quite recall, but I know it's there."

"And you feel it's important that you recall this event?"

"Yeah. My family's wellbeing may depend on it."

"Do you want to explain that further?"

"I think you probably know. My father died under...odd circumstances. Everyone in the family has been implicated in some way. None of us had anything to do with it."

"And you think this buried event might help your family prove that?"

"Honestly? I don't know. I really don't. But I feel very strongly that I need to bring it to the surface, and I need to do it now. It's tormented me for far too long."

"How so?"

"It's hard to explain."

"You're talking to a psychiatrist, Mr. Wolfe. I've heard it all. Try your best to put it into words."

"Pardon my language, but the only thing that describes it accurately is a mindfuck."

"Again, I've heard it all. Speak your mind, and don't worry about profanity. It won't upset me."

I nodded.

"Can you describe this mindfuck?"

"That's just it. I can't. But it's there. Always. I suppress it most of the time, but it never goes away. It's always there, hiding in the back of my mind, and I can't root it out. I can never find the key."

"So you want me to help you find the key."

"If there is one." I gulped. "I'm afraid there might not be a key."

There is no key.

I'd never named that painting. It was officially "Untitled by Roy Wolfe." The red backgrounds, and then the red and blue, the descent into the depths of hell. The black and dark blue, hell itself. The flecks of gold here and there, when something tried to poke its way out, but it never did.

The speck of white for...

Fuck.

A priest's collar.

That was the speck of white.

The fucking speck of white.

"Father Jim," I said.

"Who's Father Jim?"

"Our parish priest. He and my father were..." What had they been? Certainly not friends, but my father had given exorbitant amounts of money to Father Jim's ministry.

"They were what?"

"I'm not sure."

"Why did you say his name?"

"I was thinking about one of my paintings. It hangs in the lobby of our building. I've gotten offers in the seven figures for it, but I never sold it."

"Why?"

"I don't need the money."

"Have you sold other paintings?"

"Yeah. Of course."

"So why not this one?"

"It's too..."

Too what? Too personal? All my work was personal. Any artist who created something impersonal wouldn't be in business for long. Individuals had to feel something when they looked at art. If it wasn't personal to me, how could it be personal to them?

"Yes?"

"I'm not sure. I just can't sell it."

She scribbled more notes.

"Why don't you describe this painting to me."

"You can see it in the lobby of the Wolfe building."

"I can probably see it on your phone."

"Oh, yeah. Of course." I pulled my phone out of my pocket and pulled up a photo of the painting in question.

"No," she said, "that's not what I mean. I'd love to see it, but that's not what I'm after right now. I want *you* to describe it to me."

"Why?"

"Because it has meaning to you."

"All my work has meaning to me."

"Yes, but this one you've kept, despite offers of purchase. I want to hear you describe it in your own words."

I handed her my phone. "You want to look at it while I describe it?"

"Sure." She took the phone from me. "It's lovely. How big is it?"

"It's a large piece. Five by six feet."

She nodded. "All right. Describe it to me."

"The base is crimson, a bright red."

"Yes, I see. Why? What were you feeling when you painted the piece?"

"It's an older piece. I'll have to remember."

"All right. Do you want to try some guided relaxation? That might help."

My nerves sizzled along my arms. Guided relaxation. That was why I'd come, after all. Still, the thought unnerved me.

"We can continue with talking if you'd prefer," Dr. Woolcott said.

I shook my head, determined to be strong. To do what I'd come to do. "No. Let's do it."

"All right, Mr. Wolfe. Close your eyes."

43

CHARLIE

Apparently I put my career over my social life. That was what the *Cosmo* quiz indicated, anyway. No surprise there, except now I was in love with one of the owners of the business where I was employed. Still, I hadn't missed any work my first week.

Man, had it really only been a week?

It felt like a year. Not in a bad way, but so much had occurred. Now, here I was, waiting outside while one of the Wolfe heirs was in therapy.

Surreal.

Yeah, I was a little tense. My skin felt tight around my arms, and I kept rubbing at them furiously, trying to ease the shrink-wrapped feeling.

Wasn't helping.

Roy had been in with the therapist for a half hour already. I considered that a success. Half of me had expected to see him again after five minutes alone with her.

I truly hoped she could help him find whatever he was hiding so deeply within himself. Even if it didn't help us with the Derek Wolfe case, at least it would help Roy.

Roy was my priority above all else, even my job at this point. Though my job was pretty close. I mean, *Cosmo* couldn't be wrong.

I scoffed lightly at my own sarcasm as I leafed through the rest of the magazine, seeking something of substance. Nope. Not interested in creating the perfect smoky eye. Not interested in the sexual exploits of people who told their experiences to a magazine. Did people really have this much sex?

Boy, was I out of touch with reality.

Best birth control? Still not interested. The pill worked fine for me.

I finally closed the magazine and threw it back on the end table next to my chair.

Loudly, apparently, because the pretty receptionist looked up. "Can I get you anything?"

"No, thank you. I'm fine."

But I wasn't fine. I was...something. Not worried, exactly. Roy was in there with a doctor who came highly recommended. Concerned. Yeah, I was concerned.

Roy was stronger than even he knew. All the Wolfes were, having grown up with Derek Wolfe as a father. Lacey had confided in me a little while we were working on the deceased Wolfe's will. The man was ice cold. A master manipulator. A shrewd businessman with questionable ethics.

No surprise he ended up on ice.

But who had killed him? I felt certain none of his children were involved, and I knew Lacey wasn't. Yet someone out there had implicated all of them.

No arrests had been made. The Wolfe kids were simply persons of interest. Of course their fingerprints would be in his penthouse. They were his kids. They probably visited him from time to time.

Except they really didn't. They all hated him.

Still, for family functions. All but Rock had attended Derek's sixtieth birthday bash at the penthouse a week before the murder. Even Lacey had attended, as his lawyer. For their finger-prints to be there was no big deal, as far as I could see.

But I wasn't a detective. Or a lawyer.

My phone buzzed. I pulled it out of my purse. Blaine? Again?

"Excuse me," I said to the receptionist as I left the office to take the call in the hallway.

"Hello," I said nonchalantly, trying to hide the tension I felt from head to toe.

"Evening, Charlie," Blaine said. "Are you free?"

"Not really. What do you want?"

"I was wondering if the information I gave you proved valuable in any way."

"We don't know yet." Then I berated myself. Why should I tell him anything?

"I got a phone call today," he said, "from someone I think you might find interesting."

"Oh? If it's important to the case, you should contact Lacey, not me."

"Lacey and I don't have the rapport that you and I have."

I rolled my eyes and said nothing. Denying the rapport would do me no good.

He cleared his throat. "I'd like to meet you again. To give you more information."

"Why not give it to me now?"

"I don't want to use the phone. It's...delicate."

I rolled my eyes again. But the previous information he'd given me had proven fruitful, so I didn't want to waste this opportunity.

"It's late, Blaine. I can't meet you now."

"It's eight-thirty, Charlie."

"I'm...busy."

"Tomorrow evening, then. Dinner."

"Tomorrow's Saturday."

"I'm aware of that. Do you have plans?"

I hoped I did. With Roy. But the fact of the matter was Roy and I hadn't discussed it. "I'm free. What time?"

"Seven-thirty. I'll pick you up at seven."

"I'll meet you there. Text me the restaurant."

"I thought I'd make you dinner at my place."

Uh...hell, no. "No, Blaine. A restaurant or nothing."

"I guess you don't want this information, then."

Really? He was going to play that game? "I guess I don't." I was about to end the call when—

"Fine. A restaurant. I'll text you."

"Good enough."

"Goodbye, Charlie."

"Bye." This time I ended the call for real.

Another ten minutes had passed. What was going on with Roy? Before I could enter the office once more, though, my phone buzzed again.

This time it was Lacey.

"Hello?" I said, probably sounding more exasperated than I should have to my boss.

"Hey, Charlie," she said. "Sorry to bother you on Friday night."

"No bother," I said, trying to sound like I meant it. "What's up?"

"Rock got a call from Father Jim Wilkins tonight."

"Oh?"

"He said you'd been asking some odd questions."

"I only called to reconfirm the time for the memorial," I said. "We spoke for all of five minutes."

"You're not in any trouble, so don't worry," she said. "Rock hardly knows the guy—hasn't seen him in forever—but apparently Derek kept his parish going all these years."

"He's probably after more money," I said. "Now that Derek's gone, he's afraid his coffers will dry up."

Lacey laughed. "You sound just like Rock. That's almost exactly what he said verbatim."

"He volunteered some information. He told me he'd given all the Wolfe kids their first communion, and he also said Derek doted on Riley."

"Doted is hardly a fair word."

"He probably didn't know about..." I couldn't finish. Saying the words made me feel...dirty.

"Right. Are you sure that's all you talked about?"

"It was a short conversation. I didn't ask him anything. Like I said, he volunteered it.

"Good enough for me," Lacey said. "Thanks, Charlie. Again, sorry to bother you."

I walked back into the office and took my seat. The *Cosmo* still sat on the table. Nearly an hour had passed, and Roy showed no sign of coming out of Dr. Woolcott's office.

"This isn't unusual," the receptionist offered, as I glanced around the room nervously. "These late appointments often go on for an hour or so later because she doesn't have anyone else waiting.

I nodded.

This was important. I could wait.

44

ROY

The pine trees were thick in the woods. The needles bristled against my cheeks, prickling me. Though it was daylight, the trees and shadows obscured the light, and I squinted to maintain my vision.

The light ahead seemed just out of reach. Every time I got closer, another tall and narrow pine tree popped out, its branches impeding my progress.

More trees.

More trees.

More trees.

Snakelike roots protruded from the ground. I had to maneuver around them lest I trip over one and fall.

I tripped only once.

Now I had the dance down. The roots—they had a design. Once I figured out the puzzle, I could skate around them smoothly.

The trees, though. They kept popping up.

And I got colder.

The wind whipped through me, leaving icy shards on my skin.

But I wore a coat.

Weird. I didn't remember putting on a coat. But suddenly it was there, a down parka, and my arms were no longer cold, and the icy shards warmed into coziness.

Keep going, a voice said. Just keep going.

Was the voice inside my mind? It seemed to drift into me along with the wind, but it didn't sound like my voice. Didn't sound like a man at all.

It was a woman's voice.

Keep going. Keep going.

I moved along, now warm inside my parka, dancing around the roots as they presented at my feet.

But the trees. They never stopped. Never ended. Just when I thought I'd gotten closer to the light, more trees appeared. They popped up like they did in a child's storybook.

Pop. Pop. Pop.

So much to get through. So dense was this forest. So many layers to peel. So many. So many.

Onward I trudged, through the dense foliage, over the tangled roots. Warm now, clothed in the parka, the down insulation like a fire on a hearth.

Keep going. Keep going. Keep going.

I inhaled deeply, gathering my courage and my strength. Keep going, I said to myself, closing my eyes. Keep going. It's getting easier. You figured out the roots, you found a coat to keep you warm. Only the trees left to master.

Only the trees.

I opened my eyes.

A clearing. No more trees. And in the distance, a metal cube stood.

I walked toward it slowly, slowly, slowly.

Until I could see what it was.

An elevator.

A fucking elevator.

And lying on the ground in front of it was...

A key.

~

My eyes popped open.

"Mr. Wolfe?"

Where the hell was I? My arms were still warm until I regarded them. I no longer wore the parka, and goosebumps popped out from the cold. Yes, my arms were cold again. Cold like they'd been...

"Was I in a forest?" I asked.

"You seemed to be," Dr. Woolcott said.

"But why? I've never been in a forest in my life. I'm not really an outdoors person."

"You were inside your mind. Your mind created the forest as a barrier to the memory you seek. It's quite common."

"Forests?"

"Forests. Mountains. Water. All are barriers. One patient of mine actually created a black hole."

"So buried memories are common?"

"I wouldn't say common, exactly, but more common than you might think."

"Why? I finally got through the forest, finally made it to a clearing...and then pop. Here I am. Why didn't it work?"

"It did."

"But it didn't. I found the key. Actually saw it lying in front of an elevator, but then suddenly I'm back here."

"I understand your frustration, but you made great progress for your first session."

"But now I'll have to start all over."

She shook her head. "It will be easier the next time. You'll have a coat, and you already know how to get through the tapestry of roots on the ground."

"Wait. How do you know about that?"

"I was guiding you. Instructing you."

"You showed me how to get through the forest?"

"No. I simply gave you the tools to get through yourself."

"The coat?"

"I suggested it."

"You suggested it, and all of a sudden it was there? I don't understand."

"I can't make you do anything during hypnosis, Mr. Wolfe. I can only suggest. You want to get to the bottom of this. If you didn't, you would have ignored my suggestion for the coat."

"How did the coat just appear?"

"You made it appear. This isn't real life. It's in your mind. You can make anything appear in your mind. As an artist, you know that better than anyone."

"If I wanted to get there, why did I stop?"

"It's a normal response," she said. "You've buried this thing for so long that it will be difficult for you to find it. Part of you wants to take the easy route. Keep it buried. But part of you wants very much to find it, to deal with it and be rid of it. It's that part that I try to bring out of you."

"But we failed."

"Hardly. You did much better than a lot of my patients in their first session. You actually got through the barrier. That says a lot about you and your determination, Mr. Wolfe. I can't make any guarantees, but I think you're going to be successful."

"Can we go on?" I asked. "Finish this tonight?"

"You've been here for two hours. This takes a lot out of you. You need some rest."

As if on cue, my face split into a giant yawn. Right. I hadn't slept in over a day. I probably did need to rest.

"But I want to keep going. I don't want to lose it. I don't want to find myself in the forest again."

"You may very well find yourself in the forest again, but like I said, you'll have an easier time getting out."

"When can I come back?"

"We'll set something up with Nanette on the way out. I'll get you in as soon as I can."

"I'll come anytime. Money is no object."

She laughed. "Not for a Wolfe, I'm sure. I'll do my best to accommodate you." Then she stood. "Shall we?"

I followed her out of her office.

Feeling better than I had in some time.

45

CHARLIE

I jerked when the door to Dr. Woolcott's office finally opened. Roy followed her out, his eyes sunken and fatigued but oddly brighter than I'd seen them in a few days.

"Hey," I said softly.

"Hey, silver."

Dr. Woolcott walked toward the reception desk. "Nan, what do we have available in the next couple days for Mr. Wolfe?"

"You're busy all day tomorrow. There's Sunday, but that's your only day off."

"Hmm." She looked over Nan's shoulder at the computer. "I don't usually work on Saturday evenings, Mr. Wolfe, but since you did so well today I'll make an exception if you're willing to come back tomorrow, same time. Of course, I'm sure you already have plans."

We didn't. In fact, I had plans for dinner with Blaine, something I wasn't excited about conveying to Roy.

He looked to me. "You mind?"

"Of course not. If this is working, you should continue as soon as you can."

"I'll be here," he said to Dr. Woolcott.

"Great," she said. "See you both tomorrow."

See you both. She'd actually only see Roy. I had a dinner date with Blaine. Now to find the right time to let Roy know.

I smiled and took his hand, pushing Blaine to the back of my mind. "How did it go?"

"It was strange," he said. "But I think...it was good."

"That's great! You want to tell me about it?"

He paused a moment. "I'm not sure. It's not like I want to hide it from you, but I'm not sure I'm ready to talk about it."

"That's okay." I tried to sound bright, but I was a little bummed that he didn't want to talk about the session. Frankly, I found the whole thing fascinating and wanted to know more.

Maybe Lacey would be willing to talk about her session, but that wouldn't be until Monday at noon.

"What now?" I asked, as we got into a cab.

"Let's go back to my place," he said. "I want to show you the piece I've been working on."

"Wow."

Words scrambled in my mind, words of magnitude and beauty for the piece Roy showed me. But all that came out was, "Wow."

"Not everyone appreciates abstract the way you do," Roy said.

"I appreciate all art," I said. "Especially yours."

The blues and grays were haunting. They created a spiral— sort of. When I looked closer, I saw that the spiral was only an illusion. What I was actually seeing were tiny brushstrokes that all flicked downward. Quickly downward, as if someone were freefalling from the sky.

"Have you ever gone skydiving?" I asked.

"No. Why?"

"The movement of the painting. I feel like I'm falling. Falling fast."

"Yes. Falling."

"Have you ever fallen off something?"

"No," he said again.

"Hmm." What could he be saying in this painting? "Why did you paint this, Roy?"

"I felt it. So I painted it."

A-ha. Perhaps he felt like he was falling into a pit as a result of this buried memory. His attempt to find the key.

"Don't overthink it," he said.

"I'm not."

He chuckled. "You are. Your cute little forehead is all wrinkled."

When he said the words, I consciously relaxed my facial muscles. Yeah, I was overthinking it.

"Do you ever paint something without a reason?" I asked.

"Every piece of art has a reason," he said, "but it's not always something esoteric and philosophical. Sometimes, I just feel like painting, so I do."

Right. Made perfect sense. I didn't always have some deep-seated reason when I used to paint. But Roy? This painting was too engaging for him to have "just felt like painting it."

"I don't buy it."

"You don't have to buy anything."

"This is a clear descent, Roy. What does it mean?"

He wrinkled his forehead this time. "I've never fallen."

"So you've said."

"But there was one time...in an elevator..."

The elevator again. I'd seen him tense up more than once in

an elevator. And he didn't want to have sex in an elevator. Most men would jump at that.

"What happened?" I asked.

"I'm not sure, still. It's kind of blurry in my head. It might have been a dream. But I was scared shitless. It was like the floor fell out from under me."

"The cable must have broken. It happens every once in a while."

He nodded. "I swear my stomach came out through my mouth."

"You got sick?"

"No, just felt like that."

"The negative Gs," I said.

He nodded. "Yeah."

"So you don't have any desire to ride those kind of features in an amusement park, huh?"

"God, not in the slightest. The feeling of plummeting to my death isn't anything I want to relive."

I found his word usage interesting. Relive. This hadn't been a dream. Whatever happened in an elevator was part of whatever Roy had buried in his brain. Should I push it? Or should I let it go?

The fact that he'd painted this—indeed, that he'd stayed up the previous night working on it—meant it was becoming unburied in his mind.

That was a good thing, and I should probably let it happen naturally, not push.

But—

"Tell me more about the elevator, Roy."

46

ROY

The elevator.

The elevator that had appeared in the clearing after I'd trudged through the forest.

Hadn't been real, of course. I'd been under hypnosis, in a deep state of relaxation.

The gray and silver interior. Still had those same elevators. Still had...

"Roy?" Charlie said tentatively.

"I'm okay." I closed my eyes. "I want to share this with you."

"Okay."

"Except that... I didn't open it. I didn't use the key."

"What are you talking about?"

"My session. It went well, I guess."

"You said you didn't want to talk about that."

"And I don't. Except that I do."

She walked into my arms and laid her head on my shoulder. She didn't say anything, but her actions said something far more powerful than words.

She was here for me.

Had anyone ever been there for me in my life? My parents

took care of me financially, but they were hardly there for me. My father would kick my ass if I bothered him, at least until I turned sixteen and I got as big as he was. Poor Reid was his sole punching bag after that.

And my mother? She was about as attentive as that polar bear mother at the zoo who rejected her cubs.

Rock had left when I was eleven, and Reid and Riley— though I loved them, I wasn't overly close to either of them.

As an introvert, I didn't have many friends. A few dates now and then, and a few one-nighters.

No one who was there for me.

But now? I had a beautiful woman who loved me.

Heaven had sent Charlie to me. Charlie with her silver eyes. Charlie with her good heart.

She didn't push me to elaborate. She was giving me time. Time to gather my thoughts, if I even could.

Should I tell her about my trek through the imaginary forest? It almost made me sound nuts, though the doc had assured me it was very normal.

I wasn't nuts, though. I knew that, because of the elevator. Because of the key.

I'd found what I was looking for. Rather, I'd found the key to unlocking it. But at least I knew now that a key existed.

I hadn't known that before tonight.

I held onto her, relishing the warmth of her body against mine, and then I regarded my painting.

She was right.

It was a fall.

A descent.

Like that elevator had fallen on that fateful day...

∾

I SMASHED my palm onto the red button.

Then the thump when the small cubicle landed. The floor met my body, my stomach lodged in my throat.

I opened my eyes wide, attempting to see in the darkness.

No biggie. The elevator malfunctioned, obviously. Now I just needed to pry the doors open with something. But with what? Plus, I could be stuck between floors. I'd been going to the lowest floor. Had I made it?

I pushed the red button once more, and then again, until I was smashing it with my palm in a quick rhythm.

I wasn't claustrophobic, but between the darkness and the fall, I was freaking out. My heart beat like a thunderhead and I had to piss like a racehorse.

The cartons that had been on the dolly were now scattered on the floor, files tumbling out of one that had been smashed open.

A scream lodged in my throat, but I suppressed it. I wasn't going to scream like a sissy girl. My father had called me that name since I started painting, and I would not make his assessment true. For Christ's sake, he was forcing me to do this stupid internship. If that was really what he thought of me, why would he want me in his sacred office?

I lifted my hand to press the red button once more but then decided against it. Continually pushing the button was the equivalent of screaming. I'd pushed it enough already. Help would come eventually. Only the best for the Wolfes, after all.

The fucking Wolfes.

I inhaled, trying to hold it for a few seconds, and then exhaled. Breathe in, breathe out. That was supposed to relieve stress, right?

Fuck if I knew. My mother practiced a bunch of breathing exercises with her yoga. But really, it was probably just an excuse for her to get together with her other first-wife friends to bitch and whine. She even had a wine glass that had "bitch and wine" etched on it.

Odd. Thoughts of my neurotic mother actually had a calming

effect on me. Breathe in, breathe out. My eyes adjusted to the darkness
and I shoved the files back into their box. Then I stacked them all back
on the dolly. I was ready when that damned door finally—

I squinted as the light came back on.

I stood, hoping I didn't look like I'd nearly pissed myself waiting
for the elevator to move.

But it didn't move.

Instead, the doors opened.

∾

"Roy?"

I jerked out of my thoughts. Charlie had moved slightly away
and was looking into my eyes.

"Yeah?"

"Are you okay? You got kind of...rigid."

The elevator. The fall. My stomach in my throat. The fear. The
panic.

Then the lights.

The doors...

I closed my eyes, squeezing out any remainder of the
memory that threatened to come forth. No. Not now. Not now.
Not now.

I pulled Charlie back to me, enclosing her in my arms. I
drew comfort from her warmth, from her closeness.

From *her.*

"What can I do for you?" she asked, her breath a sweet
breeze on my neck.

"Just stay here. Be with me."

"I can do that."

We stood in the studio, embracing, for a long, long time.

47

CHARLIE

We didn't make love. When I finally got Roy to leave the studio, we went to the bedroom, shed our clothes, and lay down in each other's arms. He was asleep almost instantly.

Poor thing hadn't slept the night before.

I snuggled up to him, his arm around me, listening to the comfortable sound of his heartbeat.

What was it about the Wolfes?

First Lacey fell for Rock in a week, and now I fell for Roy. Would someone crawl out of the woodwork and fall for Reid next week?

I smiled to myself. What was going on with the Wolfes right now was serious. Dangerous, even, but I was happier than I could ever remember being. Crazy.

Tomorrow was Saturday, and I needed to go home. And...I needed to tell Roy I was having dinner with Blaine. That wouldn't go over well. He was going to see Dr. Woolcott, though. Did I really need to tell him? He'd be at his session for two hours, most likely. My dinner would end around the same time. We could meet back here, or at my place.

God. Was I really considering lying to Roy? That was no way to begin a relationship.

I sighed and glided my fingers over Roy's rock-hard chest and abs. His nipples tightened under my touch. I smiled again.

"WAKE UP, SILVER."

My eyes popped open. Roy was above me, his cock poised at my pussy.

"I checked. You're ready. What were you dreaming about, baby?"

I smiled. He rarely called me baby. I liked it. Silver was sweet and was only for me. It was my favorite, but something about a man calling me baby... It made me feel cherished.

Blaine had never called me baby.

And enough of that. I erased Blaine Foster from my mind and concentrated on the gorgeously handsome man about to start fucking me.

"I don't remember," I said, "but I must have been dreaming of you."

"You sure are wet." He met my gaze, his eyes smoking with desire. "I need you. I need you now."

"Then take me. I'm yours, Roy."

He thrust into me harshly. Yes, I might've woken up wet, but still the invasion burned as he tunneled into me. A good burn. The perfect burn. A burn that was meant to be.

"You feel so good," he said, his voice husky. "I swear to God, nothing has ever felt this good."

I moaned in response, unable to form words. Right now, my whole world was his cock inside me—thrusting, thrusting, thrusting—taking me home. Making me alive.

I wasn't after an orgasm, so when one crept up on me I

gasped in surprise. Simple penetration didn't usually do it for me, but he was plunging into me so hard that his pelvic bone was hitting my clit with just enough force to send me over the edge.

"I'm coming. God, Roy. I'm coming..."

"Come, baby. Please. Come for me, silver. Always come for me."

More words tumbled out of my mouth, but I didn't grasp the meaning of any of them. Only the feeling, only the pure emotion coiling within me and spreading outward, only the pure rapture and lust. I came and I came and I came, and just as I hit the peak and started floating downward, Roy thrust into me so hard, hitting my clit and sending me toppling back into the clouds once again.

"Yes," he said through clenched teeth. "Yes, God, so good."

We came together, then, not just two bodies, not just two climaxes, but two hearts and two souls.

Roy's brow was slick with sweat, and a few drops rained onto my face. His gorgeous hair was in disarray, tickling my cheeks and neck.

When he rolled off me and onto his back, I hurriedly snuggled into his shoulder, assuming the position I'd slept in all night.

"That was amazing," I said.

He didn't respond for a few seconds. Then, "*You're* amazing, silver. Everything about you is amazing."

Again, my dinner with Blaine catapulted into my mind. I wanted to erase it away, not let anything soil this beautiful moment with Roy. But I wasn't going to lie to him. Yes, I might get away with it, but it didn't feel right. It would be an ugly stain on this blooming relationship. I didn't want that.

"Roy?"

"Yeah?"

"Would it bother you if I didn't go to Dr. Woolcott's with you tonight?"

He opened his eyes and turned onto his side, meeting my gaze. "Where else would you be?"

A night with the girls. The words hovered on my tongue. They were a lie, but they would be an easy out.

Roy would know. There was no night with the girls. There were no girls. As the *Cosmo* quiz said, I put my work above my social life. Which basically meant I had no social life.

I sighed. "Blaine says he has more information for me, but he won't give it to me unless I go to dinner with him tonight."

"He doesn't have anything."

"He may not, but I can't take that chance."

"Fine, then I'll go with you."

"There's nothing I would love more than for you to come," I said. "But you can't miss your session, Roy. This is too important."

He wouldn't disagree with me.

Would he?

Though he'd told me little, the first session had been pretty successful as far as I knew.

He cleared his throat. "I won't miss my session. But I need you there with me, silver. Please."

"But—" I stopped quickly. No buts. I loved this man, and if he needed me there, I'd be there. "I'll call Blaine and cancel."

Roy nodded. He didn't look thrilled, but he looked a tad happier than he had a moment ago.

I quickly texted Blaine to let him know I wouldn't make dinner.

Lunch then? he texted back.

I thought it over for a few seconds. I had to go home anyway to change.

Okay. Noon at Luigi's.

He texted back a thumb's up, and then I sighed. Luigi's was Italian. He'd order lasagna Bolognese for me. Again.

I glanced at the time on my phone. It was already ten.

"I need to go," I said. "I want to change clothes. Plus, that red shirt... It's not that flattering."

"Are you kidding? You look amazing? Every curve is accented."

I laughed. "Yeah. That's the problem. It wasn't the most professional outfit in the world to be wearing yesterday. You want to meet for dinner before your session?"

"Sure. Just come here. I'll order something."

"Roy, we *can* actually go out in public."

"I'm not a real public person, silver. I prefer to stay in, keep my lovely lady to myself."

His words were like a warm and comforting hug. He wanted me all to himself. I liked that.

Of course, he was a classic introvert as well, so he didn't particularly enjoy being around crowds of people. Still, it was nice to hear.

"Okay. You want to pick me up at my place?"

"Of course. I'm a gentleman. I'll be happy to pick you up."

I lived in a studio apartment—tiny, but a small price to pay for actually having my own place. Now that I was making more money, I should look for something bigger. I would, but not yet. Not until I'd had this position for more than a week.

I kissed Roy goodbye—a long, lingering kiss—and went home.

Feeling kind of shady for not telling him about lunch with Blaine.

48

ROY

Charlie.

I missed her already.

I took a quick shower and returned to my bedroom to hear my phone ringing.

Hmm. I didn't recognize the area code or number.

"Yeah?" I said into the smartphone.

"Roy?"

"Shit, Riley? Where are you?"

"I'm...I don't want to say."

"I can trace this number, you know."

"By the time you do that, I'll be gone."

I couldn't trace the location anyway. Not without hanging up and making another call. I had a landline, but—

"I didn't know who else to call," my sister said.

"You can call any of us anytime."

"I hardly know Rock, and Reid... Well, he always hated me."

"That's not true." Though Reid did have a huge envy of Riley and all those trips our father took her on. He always felt, as the one who was interested in the business, that he should have been the favorite.

Now that we knew the truth, he was probably damned glad he hadn't been the favorite.

"Reid doesn't hate you. We just never knew—"

"Shit. You know now, don't you?"

"Riley, why didn't you tell us? We could have helped you. Protected you."

A pause. Then she cleared her throat. "No one could protect me. No one."

"He's gone now."

Another pause. Then, "I didn't do it, Roy."

"God, of course not," I said. "None of us think that."

"I sure had one heck of a motive, though. The cops were asking so many questions. I had to take off."

"This isn't the first time you've taken off," I said.

"I know. But the other times..."

"What about them? Why have we never been able to find you?"

"Because," she said, "Dad didn't want me found."

"But Dad was always here."

"Was he? How would you know, Roy?"

She had a point. "But Riley, you're a grown woman. You could—"

"Stop right there. Please. I've said it to myself more often than you could ever say it to me. I don't know why I let it continue. I'll never know why."

My sweet little sister needed help. So much help. Help like I was getting now. "Riley, come home. I want to help you. I've been seeing a doctor."

"Are you all right?"

"Yeah. Fine. Except in the head."

"No. Please. Tell me he didn't—"

"No. Dad didn't touch me. Other than beating the shit out of me. But Reid got it a lot worse, as you know."

"I often wonder..."

"What?"

"Whether it would have been better to have been pounded the way Reid was. Then maybe I wouldn't feel so...used."

I opened my mouth, but no words emerged. What could I say to her? Being violated in the most private way by your own father had to be worse than getting your ass kicked. I wanted to puke just thinking about it.

"What do you need, Sis?" I asked. "What can I do for you?"

"I just needed to tell someone that I'm innocent. I didn't do it."

"We know that."

"But I never said it."

"You think that ever mattered to us? We never thought you'd harm a hair on his head because—"

I stopped.

We all thought that because she was his favorite. Because he'd doted on her.

Boy, we'd been mistaken about that.

We hadn't known she had a huge motive to kill our father.

"Please, Roy. You've got to believe me."

The torment in her voice was palpable. I could feel it through the phone connection.

"I believe you," I said.

"Thanks, Roy. Tell the others, okay?"

"I will. But Ri, you need to come home."

"I can't. I just can't. Not yet."

"What about Paris? Your contract?"

"I'm a fucking mess. I can't walk a runway right now."

"You're the best, Riley. You can do it."

"I'm not the best. You should have been the model, Roy. You have more poise than I've ever had."

Huh? Since when had I had even a modicum of poise? Since the fifth of never. "You're wrong about that."

"You're quiet and reserved. You walk into a room and people can't help but be drawn to you. They can't help but want to know what makes you tick."

"Doesn't mean I'd make a good model."

"Trust me. My agent wants you."

She'd mentioned that once before, but I'd laughed it off. She'd never said anything about it again.

"I'm an artist. I draw the model. I'm not the model."

"I know. That's what I keep telling Fredricka."

"Have you talked to Fredricka lately?"

Silence for a whole minute. Seriously, I counted to sixty.

"No. I tossed my cell phone because she kept blowing it up with calls and texts."

"You're under contract," I reminded her.

"I know," she said, "and I just don't care, Roy. I just don't fucking care."

"Can I reach you again at this number?" I asked.

"No. If I want to talk to you again, I'll call you."

"At least tell me where you are. I'll be able to find the area code anyway."

"I'm not in the area code. Please. Don't try to find me. I need to..." She sighed, a whoosh into my ear through the phone. "I don't know what I need."

"Help," I said softly. "You need help."

"Not ready to face everything yet. Someday. But not now."

"Riley, please—"

"Goodbye, Roy."

"Riley, don't hang up. Don't!"

But she did.

Damn!

I did a quick search for the area code. Central Ohio. What

was in Ohio? Of course, just because the area code was in Ohio didn't mean she was in Ohio. She could have purchased a disposable cell phone there.

Or she could be using someone else's.

Damn. Damn. Damn.

My poor little sister needed help. Needed us.

But what could I do? Reid always said Riley didn't want to be found. But now...

Now she'd all but told me that she hadn't disappeared those other times. My father had taken her away.

This was all so fucked up.

My father was so fucked up.

And what was up with Father Jim? Just the thought of him had me doubling over with nausea, and I didn't have a clue why.

Except that I did.

Tonight, at my session, I was going to find out.

49

CHARLIE

I was a little late to Luigi's.

"I ordered for you," Blaine said, standing and pulling out my chair for me.

"Of course you did," I countered.

He held up the bottle of chianti that sat on the table. "Wine?"

"No thanks. I have a lot to do this afternoon." *And you know damned well I don't drink at lunch.*

"Come on, Charlie. Just one glass. It's Saturday."

"Sure."

Not that I planned to drink it. I just wanted him to shut up.

"The information you have?" I said.

"Let's have a nice lunch first. Tell me what's going on with you."

"You know what's going on with me, Blaine. We just talked two days ago."

"Nothing new?"

Only that I was twice as frustrated with him now.

I shook my head and faked taking a drink of my wine. I didn't want to play his games today. I half-agreed with Roy that this was just a fake-out, but part of me couldn't take the chance.

So I wouldn't threaten to leave if he didn't barf up the information. I'd just be quiet. Sit here. Say nothing. Answer his stupid questions with one or two words.

And wait.

I'd fucking wait.

Luckily, I didn't have to wait long.

Once our meals were delivered—freaking lasagna Bolognese yet again—he started talking.

"I'm concerned about Lacey," he said.

"Why?"

"I'm worried. The parties to that confidentiality agreement aren't nice people."

"Derek Wolfe is dead."

"But—"

"Yes, I know. You told me the other is still alive. Lacey figured out the name."

Blaine went white. "She *did*?"

I nodded. I wasn't going to say any more. If I acted like I knew the name, maybe he'd spill something.

"Don't let the collar fool you. He's not a good person."

Collar? As in a submissive's collar? *Geez, get your mind off of sex, Charlie*. A collar.

Damn.

A priest's collar.

A priest.

Father Jim.

James.

Damn.

Had I been talking on the phone with the other party to that agreement? What did they have to keep confidential? And who was the woman with an odd name?

I hoped Dr. Woolcott could help Lacey remember.

Whoever that woman was, we needed her.

"Have you been able to find the woman?" Blaine asked.

Keep cool, Charlie. Let him think you know what he's talking about.

"Not yet."

"I'd imagine she'll be difficult to find. They paid her a mint."

I nodded again, my mouth full of lasagna.

"Lacey knows this, as an attorney, but I'm going to ask you again, Charlie, to keep my name out of this. I could lose my license."

Yeah, he could. Especially since Father Jim was still alive. Derek Wolfe couldn't rise from the grave and sue Blaine for malpractice, but Father Jim sure could, and I'd bet he had plenty of cash stashed away.

"I gave you this information for a reason, Charlie," he was saying.

I swallowed. "Of course. To help Lacey."

"Yes, of course. But also because I'm so fond of you."

"I see."

"I'd like to—"

I dropped my fork onto my plate and held up my hand to stop him. "Blaine, I'm seeing someone else."

"Roy Wolfe. I know. I'm concerned. The Wolfes... They aren't good people."

"Derek Wolfe wasn't a good person. Roy Wolfe is a great person."

"Don't let all the pomp and diamonds cloud your judgment," he said. "Apples never fall far from the tree.

I stood and placed my napkin on the table. "Thanks for lunch."

"Don't go," he said. "I only meant that—"

"I know exactly what you meant. You want me to stop seeing Roy. I won't do it. I love him."

"You love him? After a few weeks?"

After one week, but I wasn't going to broadcast the fact.

"I take it that's all the information you have for me? To tell me once more not to tell anyone where I got the information? To cover your own ass?"

He cleared his throat. "Don't make a scene, Charlie."

"I won't. After all, I'd have to be here to make a scene." I walked out, a saccharine smile on my face, and hailed a cab.

I'd had more than enough of Blaine Foster for the rest of my life.

To think, I'd slept with that man! Yeah, he was good-looking, but of course he was old enough to be my father.

Eeewww!

My stomach churned. What had I been thinking?

I got into the cab, and my phone was buzzing once more. This time it was Lacey.

"Hello?" I said breathlessly.

"Charlie, it's me," she said. "Can you come to the office? I remember the woman's name."

"Okay," Rock announced. "Lace has some news, and we think it's good. Go ahead."

"I was planting marigolds in a planter today, and I thought about the marigolds and zinnias my mother used to plant every year, and it dawned on me. The woman's name. It was Zinnia!"

"That *is* unusual," Reid said.

"Exactly. I can't recall the last name, though, but now, it's like I can see the print on the document. Her first name is Zinnia."

"And you have no idea what the document is about?" Reid said.

"No. Like I told you, I only saw the signature page.

"Maybe the therapist can help you see the rest of the name," I said. "It's amazing—"

Roy darted me a look.

I cleared my throat. "What they can accomplish with hypnosis. I've been reading up."

I hadn't been about to tell them Roy had seen Dr. Woolcott, but clearly that was his fear.

"Did you happen to remember the last name of the other party?" Roy asked. "The guy named James?"

Lacey shook her head. "It's weird. I just started thinking about zinnias, and I remembered. I can't imagine there will be a time when I'm thinking about anyone's last name.

"So Dad and this James guy entered into some kind of agreement with a woman named Zinnia." Rock spoke more to himself than any of us. "I'll get the PIs on a Zinnia."

"If Dad paid her off with enough—and I'm sure he probably did—we might never find her. She could be anywhere, maybe even changed her name." Reid shuffled papers.

"Still, there will be a birth certificate on file somewhere," Lacey said. "We can begin there if nothing else surfaces. Probably not a lot of Zinnias born in New York."

"We don't know for sure she was born in New York," Reid said.

"True," Lacey agreed, "but most people tend to stay around the same area their whole life. It's a start, at least."

"The PIs will know what to do." Rock smiled at Lacey. "Good work, baby."

"I have my appointment Monday afternoon with the hypnotherapist. I might remember more. A last name would be a huge help."

I nodded. The therapist had worked wonders for Roy. I hoped she could do it for Lacey as well.

Roy spoke then. "I got a call last night. From Riley."

"Shit!" Reid nearly toppled off his chair. "That's a first. Where is she?"

"The number she called from was an Ohio area code, but she wouldn't tell me where she was."

"Why did she call?"

"She wanted to make sure we knew she was innocent," Roy said.

"None of us thought—" Reid stopped midsentence.

"Not before," Rock said, "but after I told you the truth about Dad and Riley, it crossed all of your minds."

"No." Reid shook his head vehemently.

"Not really," Roy agreed.

Reid cleared his throat. "Maybe I just didn't want to think she'd do it. She sure had a hell of a reason to."

"None of us know her very well," Roy said, "but I didn't think she could do it. Anyway, she didn't. She swears it."

"Good enough for me," Rock said.

"And me," Reid agreed.

"Still, she had a motive," Lacey said. "Probably more than any of the rest of us."

"Dad was a dick," Reid said. "I can list a hundred people who had a motive."

"None of whom are the daughter he sexually molested," Rock said.

"I wonder..." I said to myself.

"What is it, Charlie?" Lacey asked.

"Oh. Sorry. I'm not a family member. I didn't mean—"

"You're my assistant. If you have something to add, please do."

I sighed. "If he molested his daughter, isn't it possible he might have done the same thing to other girls or women?"

Four pairs of eyes met my gaze. Had that really not occurred to any of them?

"He didn't molest his sons," Reid said quietly. "Though he did beat the shit out of us."

"He liked girls," Rock said. "Not so hard to believe."

"But abusers aren't like that," Reid said. "It's not the gender that matters. It's the violation. The power."

"Some abusers like men, some like women, and some like both. Makes sense to me." Lacey cocked her head. "God, did I just say this sick shit makes sense to me?"

"We all know what you meant, Lace." Rock stood and paced around the conference table. "This Zinnia. If she were Riley's age..."

"She had to be over eighteen to sign a legal document," Lacey said.

"And this happened when you were a new associate, right?" Rock said.

Lacey nodded. "Like my second week."

And that was about six years ago. I calculated quickly. "Assuming Zinnia was young, only eighteen or nineteen, she'd be in her mid-twenties today."

"That's a big assumption," Reid said.

"I don't know that it is," Rock said. "He abused Riley. What billionaire is going to go out looking for old women?"

"True," Lacey said. "At least we've narrowed the parameters a bit."

"We'll leave it to the PIs," Rock said. "Damn, we're spending a lot of money trying to ferret out Derek Wolfe's killer when none of us are even remotely unhappy that he's gone."

"This has our father's stench all over it," Reid said.

"A setup?" Rock asked. "I wouldn't put it past him. He had all the money in the world to cover his tracks."

Roy stayed silent.

I watched him, his full lips flattened almost into a line.

He didn't believe Derek had set his kids up. He didn't believe Derek Wolfe had orchestrated his own death.

Neither did I.

"Seems like a stretch," Lacey finally said. "Derek lived the life of a king. Why would he want to end his own life and frame everyone close to him?"

"You all know him better than I do," Rock said. "But it doesn't seem like a stretch to me."

"Me either," Reid agreed.

Again, Roy stayed silent.

I'd ask him about it later.

"At least we know Riley is okay," Rock added. "That's something."

"But she won't come home," Roy said.

"Who can blame her?" Reid said.

"She's under contract." Roy pushed a strand of hair out of his eye. "She could ruin her career."

"As long as I stay at the helm of Wolfe Enterprises," Rock said, "the company is ours. Riley won't ever need to worry about money."

"You want our sister to be an heiress for a living?" Roy said. "She's much more Ivanka Trump than Paris Hilton. She should be using her brain."

"And you know this because..."

"Because she's my sister. Reid and I were around as she grew up."

"He's right, Rock," Reid said. "We may not know our sister very well, but one thing we do know is that Riley likes making her own way. It's why she got into modeling. We all know she didn't need the cash. In fact, it wouldn't surprise me if she'd like to get far away from the Wolfe money. Seems you could understand that."

"Hell, yeah, I can understand that. I'm just saying she doesn't need to worry about money. None of us do."

"Riley seemed to intimate..." Roy's voice drifted off.

"Intimate what?" Rock demanded.

"That those other times she disappeared were Dad's doing, that he..." Roy cleared his throat.

No one responded for a minute. How could we? We all knew exactly what he meant.

"I don't think I can ever forgive myself," Roy continued. "How were we so blind to what was going on, Reid?"

Reid shook his head. "I don't know. We hated the bastard, and we hated her for being his favorite."

"I never hated her," Roy said.

"You know what I mean." Reid shook his head. "We had our own issues."

"If you want to blame someone," Rock said, "blame me. I knew what was going on, and I stayed away."

Lacey touched Rock's arm. "Honey, you were stuck in military school."

"Not once I turned eighteen. I hated the bastard so much that I vowed never to return to New York again. I didn't stop to think about what I was leaving behind, the life I was condemning my baby sister to."

"You were angry," Lacey said.

"Hell, yes. Still am. But I put myself above my baby sister. That will never happen again. If it's the last thing I do, I'm going to figure out who killed that motherfucker father of ours so this shadow over all our heads disappears."

"Right there with you, bro," Reid said.

"Me too," Roy said, his dark eyes on fire.

I knew that look. I'd seen it when he and I were passionate.

It meant one thing.

He was passionate about solving this mystery. For his sister. For his brothers. For himself.

For us.

I smiled at him.

"I love you," I mouthed.

50

ROY

W armth surged through me.

Charlie loved me.

Her love gave me strength I never knew I had. Never dreamed I had. This was important. I believed with all my heart and soul that none of my siblings were responsible for my father's death. I didn't have a clue who was, but I knew without a doubt four people—five, including Lacey—who weren't.

I'd leave Zinnia to Rock, Reid, and the PIs. I had other fish to fry, namely, my therapy session this evening.

I'd made it through the forest. I'd uncovered the key.

Now all I had to do was open the door.

I ENTERED *the forest already clad in the down parka.*

I danced over the twigs.

Two obstacles down.

But the trees...

They still popped up everywhere. Just when I thought I'd made it back to the clearing, another tree stood in my way.

Tall pine trees, whose needles pricked my skin, causing red bumps to erupt.

I gazed at my hands. They itched and burned. Damn! I rubbed furiously at them, my skin peeling away.

No. I loved pine trees! I loved visiting upstate New York where they flourished in the Adirondacks.

I wasn't allergic. Why were they making my skin red and swollen with pricks and boils?

I picked up my pace, panting, my hands throbbing as the pine resin inflamed them.

No. Didn't make sense. Didn't make sense.

The pain stopped.

I regarded my hands. The boils and scratches were gone. Yes!

But still more trees stood in my way.

Trees... Trees... Trees...

Until they were gone.

And I stood once more in the clearing.

The steel cube stood in the distance.

The elevator.

I ran.

And I ran.

And I ran.

Yet the elevator seemed to be getting farther and farther away.

Until I stopped abruptly, the steel wall only a foot away from me.

On the mossy ground lay the key.

Pick it up.

Was that my voice? No, it was my head. Someone had planted the words in my head.

Perhaps that someone was me.

Was I ready?

I didn't move, and the key stayed in place.

For so long I'd buried this memory under layers and layers of steel in my mind.

The roots, the cold, the tree—all were barriers I'd created.

I'd made it through the barriers.

Only this last barrier—this key—remained.

Pick it up.

The words again.

I bent over and grasped the key. The metal was hot against my flesh, so hot I nearly dropped it. Metal should be cool, not hot. I inhaled.

An acrid scent of burnt flesh.

The key fell from my hand, and in my palm, a sizzling red burn in the shape of it remained.

No!

No!

I bent over and picked it up again, determined to see this through. It still burned my hand, but I didn't care. I slipped it in the keyhole above the elevator pad.

Turned it.

The elevator doors slid open.

And I entered.

51

CHARLIE

I sat in the waiting area. I'd leafed through another issue of *Cosmo* and was now looking at *People*.

Roy hadn't talked much at dinner, and I hadn't told him about my lunch with Blaine. Didn't matter. Nothing had been accomplished, anyway, and Blaine knew now where I stood. Of course, I'd made it clear before, and that hadn't stopped him.

I sighed.

The receptionist looked up. "Do you need anything?"

I shook my head. "Sorry. I'm just a little antsy."

"I'm sure he's doing fine."

I smiled and gave a slight nod. I was sure he was doing fine as well. I was just nervous about what was about to be revealed.

What it might mean for Roy.

I loved Roy Wolfe. I loved him more than I ever thought it was possible to love another human being. I wanted the best for him. I wanted him free from pain. I wanted whatever had been tormenting him out of his head.

He deserved to live a normal life. Well, as normal a life as any heir to a fortune could live. Together, though, he and I could be happy. Have something close to normal. Next to normal, at least.

I bit my lip, picked up my phone, read through a few emails, and then grabbed another magazine.

Dr. Woolcott had promised to stay as late as necessary tonight.

I had a feeling I'd be here for a while.

52

ROY

Get in.

That voice again. The voice that was mine but not mine.

Get in.

Get in the elevator.

I looked at my palm. The burn from the key had miraculously healed.

Get in.

I walked forward. One. Two. Three steps. Then one more. I stood, steel walls on three sides. And the doors closed slowly, slowly, slowly.

Now what?

The panel had only one button. The red one. The one you pressed in an emergency.

The one I'd pressed when...

When...

When...

Press the button.

Press the button.

Press the button.

My hand shook as I lifted it to the red button pulsing along with my heart.

I pressed it.

"Fuck!" I screamed.

My body plunged along with the steel trap that encased me. My stomach rose through my body, lodging in my throat.

The boxes. The dolly. I remembered.

They were there. One had been smashed open, and files were strewn over the floor.

I stood, fighting off the shivers, and picked up the files, placing them back in the carton.

Then the doors parted.

And—

~

I SHOT MY EYES OPEN.

"Mr. Wolfe?"

I turned toward the voice. Dr. Woolcott's face was a blur. The whole room was a blur.

And I remembered.

I fucking remembered.

"A woman. Very young. Blond. She was naked. Her skin was... She'd been cut. Cuts on the top of her breasts, trickles of red blood oozing down over her nipples. Her...

How could I have forgotten this?

"Easy," Dr. Woolcott said. "Take it slowly."

"My father's office. I was taking cartons of files down to the lower level for storage. I was eighteen. No, nineteen, doing an internship. The elevator stopped. Then the shaft broke, and it fell. It fell. But LL was the lowest level in the building. I know it went down. I don't understand. I don't..."

"Maybe there was a floor below the lowest floor," the doctor said.

"Yeah. Yeah, there must have been."

"Tell me more about the girl."

"She was young, I think. Around my age. Maybe even younger. She gasped. She was saying 'Help me. Please help me.'" Then...blank.

"I don't remember anything after that." I rubbed my forehead. "Damn! The woman! What happened to the woman?"

"Concentrate. Do you want to go back under?"

I nodded. "Yeah. It's the only way."

No barriers this time. *The elevator doors opened as I collected the strewn files.*

A naked woman ran toward me. "Help me! Please, help me!"

"What? Who are you?" I looked into the dark hallway. "Where is this?"

"Please." She gulped, tears streaming down her face. "Get me out of here." She frantically pushed buttons on the panel.

"Damn it! Shut, you fucking door. Shut!"

The doors didn't move. I quickly removed my shirt and wrapped it around her shoulders, her blood soaking into the stark white fabric. She was shivering, so frightened.

"What happened to you?" I asked.

"Just get me out of here. Get me out of here!"

This time I began punching at the buttons. Move, damn it. Move! Then footsteps.

"No!" She gasped. "No! They're coming."

"Who? Who's coming?"

"They want to... They tried to..." She burst into sobs. "Please. Please get me out of here!"

Then a voice. "We know you're around here somewhere, bitch. Don't try to hide."

I knew that voice.

That voice had been raised to me many times.

My father.

"Who are you?" I said. "What did he do to you?"

"Not he. They. They're going to kill me. Please, get me out of here."

"I'm trying."

"It's a game," she said. "They're playing a game."

A game? My father? They? Who were the others?

"What kind of game?"

"A hunting game. And I'm the prey."

MY EYES SHOT open once more. "God, I remember now. I remember."

"Take it slow, Mr. Wolfe. What do you remember?"

Get out of here! This has nothing to do with you! Go do your sissy art!

"My father. He came running through the dark hallway, and behind him was..." I gulped. "Our priest. Father Jim."

CHARLIE

Roy's eyes were circled with shadows when he emerged from Dr. Woolcott's office.

"We need to get everyone together," he said to me. "Now."

I nodded. I didn't even think of questioning him. His eyes were dead serious.

AN HOUR later we were back in the conference room where we'd sat during the afternoon to get Lacey's news about Zinnia.

I, along with Rock, Reid, and Lacey, heard Roy's story for the first time.

"How could you have kept that inside for so long?" I asked.

"I don't know," Roy said. "I buried it so deep, I guess. All this time, I knew there was something in there, something fucking with my mind, but I kept it buried, let it come out in my artwork. The only way I could deal with it."

"Did our father do something to you?" Rock asked. "Something to make you forget?"

"I wouldn't put it past him." Reid stroked his chin.

"I don't know. It's clear as day now." Roy rubbed at his temples. "Dad and Father Jim came running toward the elevator, and..." He closed his eyes. "Finally, the doors shut. All that time I'd been trying to get them to close, but they wouldn't. Then, just in the nick of time, they did. That's all I remember until..." He squeezed his eyes shut harder.

"Until what?" Reid asked.

"I remember going up in the elevator. I remember the door opening into the lobby. I remember the girl running out screaming. Then it all went black."

"You probably fainted."

"No. I didn't faint." Roy rubbed the back of his head. "I woke up later with a throbbing headache and a bump on the back of my head."

"Someone knocked you out," Rock said, "and I'll bet you the Wolfe fortune I know who."

"It couldn't have been Dad," I said. "He was somewhere else. Down..."

"Are you saying there's a lower floor to our building that none of us know about?" Reid asked.

"I don't know what I'm saying. All I know is the elevator shaft broke and I fell. When the doors opened, I didn't recognize where I was. And there wouldn't be a naked woman running around on any of the other floors. Dad was down there. He couldn't have been the one who hit me."

"So there's Dad, Father Jim, and some unknown assailant," Rock said, shaking his head.

"And the woman," Lacey added. "Whatever they planned for her, she escaped it. None of you ever heard anything more about this?"

"I wasn't around," Rock said.

"And I never heard a thing," Reid added. "I don't even remember you having a concussion, Roy."

"Neither do I, really," Roy said.

"A concussion can sometimes cause some retrograde amnesia," I piped in. "Maybe that's what happened to you, Roy."

"Or Derek could have drugged you," Lacey offered. "A lot of drugs can make you lose the several hours before you actually took them."

"Maybe," Roy said. "Dad couldn't have let me remember. What if I'd gone to the authorities? He'd have been finished."

"Or not," Rock countered. "He probably *owned* the authorities."

"Then how could he be remembering now?" Reid asked. "No, this was something he buried intentionally. What that detective said is starting to make sense."

"What?" Roy asked, still rubbing his head.

"Hank Morgan. He said some of your artwork showed signs of psychosis."

Roy stood. "*What?*"

"Relax." Rock's voice was oddly soothing. "We didn't believe it. We *don't* believe it."

Reid nodded. "I only mean that it makes sense that some of your art is dark. It must be how you dealt with this all these years."

Roy sat back down and rubbed his forehead. "My painting. The one in the lobby... I know what it means now. I found the key."

I smiled, wishing I could take him in my arms and comfort him.

"It doesn't matter how or why you remembered," Lacey said. "It only matters that you did."

She was right. Roy would be okay now. The road might be dark and bumpy, but he'd be okay. And I'd be at his side.

"In the meantime," Lacey continued, "I guess we find this secret lower level in this building."

Icy bumps erupted on my arms. We sat in a building with a secret.

A big secret.

"First thing next week," Rock said, "we're bulldozing this motherfucker to the ground."

"We can't," Reid said.

"The hell we can't."

"Dad had a way in," Reid said. "We'll find that. My guess is he isn't the only one who knew how to get in."

"Father Jim?" I asked.

"Maybe. If Dad trusted him with that knowledge." Reid loosened his tie.

Why was he wearing a tie on Saturday?

"Well," Lacey said, "this all has to wait until after the memorial service next week. You all need that to happen to make it look like you give a shit the bastard's dead."

Reid nodded. "Plus, Father Jim will be there. Give us a chance to get information out of him while he's not on guard."

Roy tensed visibly at Father Jim's name. So did I.

"We have a week." Roy stood, his countenance still rigid. "Then we find whatever our dead father is hiding here and put an end to this hell once and for all." He turned to me. "Let's go."

"Are we done here?" I asked Lacey.

"Yeah. Go home. Take tomorrow for yourself. You deserve it. Next Friday is the memorial. We'll all need our energy to get through it."

I took Roy's hand that he held out to me. I guessed it was old news now. Roy and I were together.

And I wouldn't have it any other way.

~

BACK AT ROY'S PLACE, I wanted to give him something special. Show him what he meant to me. I led him into his studio to my watercolor that was still covered.

"You don't have to," he said.

"I want to. Just don't be disappointed, okay?"

"You could never disappoint me, silver. Never."

I nodded, hoping against hope he spoke honestly. I had a tiny percentage of the talent Roy had. I grasped the cloth covering but then froze.

"You okay?" Roy asked.

"Yeah. But I need to ask you something."

"Sure."

"Your brothers both seem to think your father might have been behind his own murder."

"Yeah." He cleared his throat. "They made that clear."

"Yet you said nothing. Do you agree with them?"

Roy didn't answer right away. His gaze rested on the covered watercolor. Finally, "No, I don't agree with them. My father didn't take his own life."

"I see. Why do you think that?"

His dark eyes gazed at something intangible. "Because he was a megalomaniac, silver. Obsessed with his own power. What he could do. How he could spit in the face of the laws, of other people's rights. In his mind, he was a god, and gods don't kill themselves, even to screw their children over."

I touched his cheek. "Why don't your brothers see that?"

"Because they don't know what I know. Haven't seen what I've seen."

"But you told them all about your repressed memories."

"I did. But they didn't live it. I did. And I have a glimpse inside my father that they don't. Even Riley, as much as she went through at his hands. She never saw what I saw. What he was truly capable of. How many women were hunted, tortured, and then died for my father's little game? For his amusement?"

I nodded, suppressing the nausea. My stomach knotted. I wanted desperately to leave this horrible place. Didn't want to think about what Derek Wolfe's victims had suffered. I had to, but not now.

Besides, Roy had said it all.

"I'm going to be okay now," he said. "I know it."

"You will be. I'll see to it." I braced myself and removed the cloth from my watercolor. "Please don't hate it.

He gazed upon my work, and a smile edged onto his lips. "You made me whole, silver. You made me whole."

I stood beside him and regarded my own work, tried to see it through his eyes.

"I love it," he said. "You gave my face a serene look. Somehow you show me relaxed in a way I've never been. You made me whole in this painting. And in every other way. Come here."

I turned into his arms and met his lips in a soft kiss.

"I love you, Charlie," he said.

"I love you too, Roy. So much." I snuggled against his hard shoulder. "We'll figure this out. Together."

EPILOGUE
RILEY

The beauty of being my father's daughter was that he'd taught me from a young age to be a proficient liar. I could convince anyone of anything. All I had to do was smile, flutter my eyes a little, and wiggle my ass when I walked away.

Worked great on the runway.

All eyes on me.

Except when I wanted to disappear.

My father had taught me that, as well.

Not only could I make the marks on my skin—courtesy of the bastard—disappear, I could disappear wholly.

Usually at his behest. This last time?

All me.

He was gone. Burning in the flames of hell, I hoped.

Still he saw me. I felt his nauseating gaze on my body, his clammy touch on my flesh. That's why I burned myself sometimes.

After all, I'd been taught well how to hide scars.

Sometimes, though, even burning didn't help.

Sometimes, I wasn't sure anything ever would.

WOLFES OF MANHATTAN continues with *Runaway*, coming soon!

A NOTE FROM HELEN

Dear Reader,

Thank you for reading *Recluse*. If you want to find out about my current backlist and future releases, please visit my website, like my Facebook page, and join my mailing list. If you're a fan, please join my street team to help spread the word about my books. I regularly do awesome giveaways for my street team members.

If you enjoyed the story, please take the time to leave a review. I welcome all feedback.

I wish you all the best!

Helen

Facebook

Facebook.com/helenhardt

Newsletter

Helenhardt.com/signup

Street Team

Facebook.com/groups/hardtandsoul

ACKNOWLEDGMENTS

Thank you so much to my editor, Celina Summers; my proof-reader, Christie Hartman; my beta readers, Martha Frantz, Theresa Finn, Karen Aguilera, Angela Tyler, and Linda Pantlin Dunn; and my cover artists, Kim Killion and Marci Clark. You all helped *Recluse* shine!

ALSO BY HELEN HARDT

Steel Brothers Saga:

Trilogy One—Talon and Jade

Craving

Obsession

Possession

Trilogy Two—Jonah and Melanie

Melt

Burn

Surrender

Trilogy Three—Ryan and Ruby

Shattered

Twisted

Unraveled

Trilogy Four—Bryce and Marjorie

Breathless

Ravenous

Insatiable

Trilogy Five—Brad and Daphne (coming soon)

Fate

Legacy

Descent

Follow Me Series (coming soon):

Follow Me Darkly

ABOUT THE AUTHOR

#1 *New York Times*, #1 *USA Today*, and #1 *Wall Street Journal* best-selling author Helen Hardt's passion for the written word began with the books her mother read to her at bedtime. She wrote her first story at age six and hasn't stopped since. In addition to being an award-winning author of romantic fiction, she's a mother, an attorney, a black belt in Taekwondo, a grammar geek, an appreciator of fine red wine, and a lover of Ben and Jerry's ice cream. She writes from her home in Colorado, where she lives with her family. Helen loves to hear from readers.

http://www.helenhardt.com

CPSIA information can be obtained
at www.ICGtesting.com
Printed in the USA
LVHW020315290721
693949LV00005B/438